# BOOKS BY A.D. STARRLING

### Seventeen Novels

Hunted

Warrior

Empire

Legacy

Origins

Destiny

### Seventeen Short Stories

First Death

Dancing Blades

The Meeting

The Warrior Monk

The Hunger

The Bank Job

### Legion

Blood and Bones

Fire and Earth

Awakening

Forsaken

Hallowed Ground

Heir

Legion

Witch Queen

The Darkest Night

Rites of Passage

Of Flames and Crows

Midnight Witch

A Fury of Shadows

Witch Queen

The Incubus and The Bodyguard

Seventeen Universe

The Party

Diary of a Reluctant Werewolf

It All Started With A Bite

How to Stake a Vampire

Division Eight

Mission:Black

Mission: Armor

Mission:Anaconda

Miscellaneous

Void - A Sci-fi Horror Short Story

The Other Side of the Wall - A Horror Short Story

# A.D. STARRLING

## HOW TO STAKE A VAMPIRE

# DIARY OF A RELUCTANT WEREWOLF

### BOOK 2

# COPYRIGHT

# DEAD-SERIOUS BUSINESS

Dear Diary,

It's been three weeks since I became a werewolf. I'm about to attend my first meeting with the Amberford Alliance. Victoria has briefed me seventeen times on proper etiquette, Pearl has critiqued my outfit choices until my ears bleed, and Samuel keeps giving me looks that suggest he's already planning my funeral.

Apparently, the last time someone "disrupted" an Alliance meeting, half of downtown ended up on fire. So, no pressure.

FYI, I resent the fact that everyone assumes I'm going to cause some kind of incident.

…Okay, they're probably right…

Abigail West

(99% confident I'm about to put my foot in my supernatural mouth.)

"Remember," Victoria said for the eighteenth time as we headed for the Chamber of Commerce, "you are here to observe and learn. Don't look anyone in the eye and don't speak unless directly addressed."

"And if you *are* addressed," Pearl instructed curtly from Victoria's arms, "try not to insult anyone's ancestry, dietary habits, or personal hygiene."

"That was one time," I muttered.

"It was three times," Samuel corrected. He adjusted his tie with a stiff movement that did little to calm my nerves. "And one of them was literally yesterday."

I shot him a narrow-eyed look and did my best to ignore how hot he looked in his suit.

"How was I supposed to know asking the banshee at the dry cleaners about her vocal cord maintenance routine was considered rude?"

Samuel sighed. "Because normal people don't ask banshees about their vocal cords."

I decided not to point out that no one in our group was normal.

"Well, excuse me for being curious about supernatural anatomy," I grumbled instead, smoothing down my dress. It was one of Claudette's creations and had cost more money than I cared to know about. "Besides, I thought you liked my curiosity."

The heated look Samuel gave me made my face grow warm and reminded me exactly how much he appreciated certain aspects of my curiosity.

Unfortunately, it also reminded me of this morning's argument about our living arrangements.

"You're being unreasonable," he'd said, pacing around the Hawthorne mansion kitchen like a bear who'd woken up early from his hibernation. "We're mated. Tradition dictates you live with me."

"Tradition can kiss my ass," I'd shot back irritably where I was eating toast at the breakfast bar. "I'm not giving up my independence just because some cosmic wolf magic decided we're compatible."

The fact was we were more than compatible. The mate bond made every touch electric and every night together feel like the world was ending in the best possible way. But that wasn't the point. The point was I'd spent my entire adult life being self-reliant and I wasn't about to hand over the keys to Samuel Hawthorne, no matter how ridiculously gorgeous he looked in and out of a suit or how he made my toes curl when he—

Victoria cleared her throat. "Perhaps we could save the mating displays for after the meeting?"

"We weren't—" I started.

"You were." Pearl curled a lip. "Your pheromones are practically nauseating."

"Also, you both smell like you want to do that thing with the handcuffs again," Bo added with his usual lack of tact.

Samuel choked on air. Victoria went pale. Pearl looked like she was considering becoming a vegetarian just to avoid being associated with carnivores.

"Bo!" I hissed, heat crawling up my neck.

"What?" The Husky side-eyed me and wagged his tail innocently. "I'm just saying what everyone's thinking."

"No one was thinking that," Samuel muttered, his face red behind his glasses.

"I was," Bo contributed cheerfully. "Abby gave me extra treats that day."

My belly clenched when I met Samuel's hot gaze. We'd both really enjoyed the handcuffs.

Luckily, I was distracted by the looming building we were approaching.

The Amberford Chamber of Commerce looked like someone had taken a respectable colonial building and gone to town with the embellishments. The original redbrick facade was populated with gargoyles along the roofline and there were enough decorative cornices and pediments on the thing to make an architecture professor faint in horror.

I eyeballed the assortment of vehicles in the parking lot we were crossing with a degree of dread.

A sleek black hearse sat next to a Bentley with tinted windows so dark they were probably illegal. A vintage Rolls-Royce that looked like it belonged in a museum was parked beside a monster of a motorcycle. A pink Cadillac huddled beside a midnight-blue Bugatti.

Bo panted noisily beside me, his face alight with the unhealthy glow of automobile adoration.

"He watched a show on vintage cars again last night," I explained at the others' stares.

Samuel rolled his eyes. By now, the entire

Hawthorne pack knew about Bo's addiction to the Discovery channel.

"Maybe you should buy him a toy car," Pearl suggested in the casual tone of someone who'd never worked for a dime in her life.

Bo studied me hopefully.

I frowned. "You're afraid of the vacuum cleaner."

"A vacuum cleaner is not a car," my dog shot back wisely. He stiffened and sniffed the air as we neared the entrance to the Chamber of Commerce. His tail drooped. "This place smells like a funeral home." He moved closer to me.

"Some of the Alliance members are old," Pearl declared with a swish of her tail.

That wasn't sinister at all. An ominous creak distracted me from my spiraling thoughts of doom.

A doorman who looked like he moonlighted as a bouncer at an exclusive club was opening the heavy oak doors for us. His scent marked him as a werewolf. He wore a bored look that suggested he'd seen enough supernatural politics and drama in his lifetime to remain permanently unimpressed by anything short of an actual apocalypse.

His expression changed when he saw me. He visibly paled.

I swallowed a sigh.

My reputation as a white luna had been making the rounds in Amberford's supernatural community. I had to admit I wasn't exactly crazy about my newfound fame. It made for awkward situations and even more awkward conversations. It didn't help that I had incapacitated the cream of Amberford's society a short while back with a single command and everyone was now busy pretending that never happened.

A discreet brass plaque beside the main doors read *Amberford Chamber of Commerce: Serving Our Community Since 1868.* My gaze landed on the small inscription beneath it.

It said *All Species Welcome.*

No doubt that one was only visible to supernatural creatures.

"Good evening, Mrs. Hawthorne," the doorman said with a skittish nod. "The Alliance is gathering in the *Twilight Conference Room.*" He glanced nervously at my hands, as if expecting to see the crystal skull I had used to immobilize Amberford's supernatural elite at the now-infamous Holt ball.

I gave the guy a friendly smile. He gulped, Adam's apple bobbing wildly and eyes darting sideways as if looking for an escape route.

"Maybe try not to smile at anyone when we're in the conference room," Victoria suggested diplomatically as we entered the building.

I sagged a little. Samuel patted my arm.

This was going to be a long night.

The lobby was grand and what you'd expect from a building that hosted both human business meetings and supernatural summits. Tasteful artwork lined the walls and expensive rugs covered polished hardwood floors. A crystal chandelier cast warm light over leather furniture that looked like it had been designed for both comfort and confidentiality.

But what caught my attention and drew me up short were the smells. Layers of supernatural scents danced in the air, creating a complex bouquet that made my enhanced nose twitch. Vampires, werewolves, witches, fae, dwarves, pixies, dragon newts, and things I couldn't yet identify all mingled together in an olfactory signature that screamed "powerful people making important decisions."

Bo whined softly and pressed against my leg.

"You two okay?" Samuel asked quietly.

"I will be," I said with more confidence than I felt.

"Do try not to embarrass us," Pearl warned as we headed toward a grand staircase at the far end of the lobby. "That goes for you too, mutt."

Bo looked like he'd changed his mind about tagging along for this meeting.

Dark wood banisters gleamed under the glow of sconces as we started up the stairs, the carpet runner thick enough to muffle our footsteps. The portraits lining the walls featured stern-faced individuals in period dress who looked like they'd rather be anywhere else but here. Several of them appeared to be tracking our progress with their painted eyes, which was either expensive magical art or weird regular art.

"That's creepy," Bo quavered.

"Are those...?" I trailed off and indicated the portraits.

"Former Alliance leaders," Samuel confirmed quietly. "Some of them are still around, technically."

I grimaced. "Technically?"

"Vampire politics are complicated," Victoria said.

Bo's claws clicked on hardwood as we reached the second-floor landing. A long hallway stretched before us. It was lined with doors bearing brass nameplates: *Committee Room A, Private Dining, Archive Storage,* and, most ominously, *Disciplinary Hearing Room.*

"Please tell me that last one isn't for people who ask too many questions," I muttered.

Victoria and Samuel's silence did little to reassure me.

The hallway culminated in a pair of mahogany doors. A nameplate read *Twilight Conference Room* in elegant script.

The hairs on the back of my neck rose at the powerful smells coming from inside it.

Victoria straightened her already perfect posture, a determined expression on her face. Pearl moved her tail with lazy arrogance. Bo braced like he intended to bolt at the first sign of danger.

Samuel steeled himself and opened the doors.

## 2

# THE ROUND(ISH) TABLE
# OF DOOM

My first impression of the *Twilight Conference Room* was that the place lived up to its name.

The ornate crystal chandelier suspended from the central ceiling seemed to be mostly for show since the muted light barely dappled the shadows in the far corners. The floor was dominated by a massive oval table surrounded by chairs that looked like they'd been designed to make their occupants feel important. The walls were dotted with expensive-looking artwork and portraits of more ominous and possibly constipated people.

Add in a few votive candles and a crystal ball and the place could have passed for a phony psychic's lair.

My gaze landed on the figures seated around the table. I recognized a few faces from the tea party at Château Montmartre. Still, there were plenty of new ones that made my wolf sit up and take notice.

Gregory and Constantia Tremaine sat near the head

of the table, looking like vampire royalty in their perfectly tailored clothes. Constantia stiffened fractionally when we entered the room, her crimson-tinged gaze assessing me guardedly. Considering the state my powers had left her in at the Holt ball, I wasn't exactly surprised.

"Ah, the Hawthornes." Gregory greeted us with a smile that didn't quite reach his eyes. "Please, join us. We were just discussing tonight's agenda."

A woman with silver hair pulled back in a severe chignon looked up from her notes where she sat to his right. She wore an expensive navy suit and had the kind of razor-edged features that suggested she either ate children for breakfast or regularly foreclosed on orphanages for fun.

"You must be Abigail West." She rose as we approached the table, her smile sharp enough to cut glass. The scent of magic drifting off her marked her as a witch. "I'm Daria Tilcott, the Alliance chair." She came around and offered me her hand.

I heard several faint inhales just beyond the point of normal human hearing, the loudest of them Victoria's. A protective feeling mixed with anxiety hummed across the mate bond from Samuel as he took a step closer to me. Pearl's eyes shrank to slits. Bo gulped noisily.

The silence deepened until you could have heard a pin drop.

This was evidently some sort of test.

I eyed the woman's hand before taking it. "Please, call me Abby."

Surprise darted briefly in Daria's dark eyes, so quick I would have missed it were it not for my wolf's senses. She watched me with an inscrutable expression. "How refreshing." Her handshake was firm and brief. "I must admit I have yet to meet a Hawthorne as friendly as you are." She glanced pointedly at a stony-faced Victoria and a tight-lipped Samuel before turning a steady gaze on Bo. "I hear he's part werewolf."

"Which part?" someone muttered from the shadows.

Bo ignored the insult and wagged his tail hesitantly where he stuck to my side like glue. "You smell like engine oil."

Daria blinked, apparently disarmed by my four-legged goofball's charm. "My broomstick is getting repaired, so I had to ride the bike tonight."

Bo brightened, his tail speeding up. "You mean the Harley is yours? Cool!"

Daria arched an eyebrow. "You know what a Harley is?"

"Yeah. Just so you know, I'd never barf on one. Unlike Marshmallow."

Daria's eyes glazed over a little. "Who's Marshmallow?"

"The Saint Bernard who lives the next street over from our apartment," I explained.

"He's a butt sniffer," Bo added helpfully.

Someone choked in the gloom.

I clocked Victoria and Samuel's accusing stares. "In Bo's defense, Pearl didn't teach him Alliance etiquette."

We looked at the cat.

Pearl flicked her tail irritably. "What?"

Victoria guided us to a cluster of empty chairs before I or my dog could say more socially incriminating things. Daria looked a little relieved as she returned to her seat.

I finally got my first good look at the rest of the Alliance.

Portia O'Keefe, the head of the Amberford banshees, nodded a regal acknowledgment across from us. Her expression indicated we were never to mention what had happened at the Holt ball in her presence.

Next to her was a man I didn't recognize. He was tall, pale, and had eyes that suggested he'd seen empires rise and fall, probably while complaining about property taxes the entire time.

Victoria introduced him. "That's Cornelius Heathwood, head of the fae."

Cornelius inclined his head with otherworldly grace. "Ms. West. Your reputation precedes you."

"Trust me, I wish it didn't," I said levelly.

"On the contrary," a melodious voice said from farther down the table. "Reputations can be quite useful, when they are properly managed."

The speaker was a stunning woman who looked like she'd stepped out of a Renaissance painting. All flowing auburn hair, wispy dress, and ethereal beauty, her scent indicated she was fae too. But there was something else there. An undertone that made my wolf pay attention.

"Melody Flowers." She introduced herself with a

smile that was probably illegal in several states. "I'm temporarily representing the local covens."

This earned her a wary side-eye from Portia and several other Alliance members.

"What happened to the Lincoln sisters?" Victoria asked, unable to hide her surprise.

"They're out of town," Melody replied smoothly. "It seemed recent events were too taxing for them. We decided they needed a well-deserved…break."

I swallowed. The way she said "break" made it sound like the Lincoln sisters had been fed through a wood chipper. Judging from Samuel's frown, he was thinking the same thing.

I was beginning to understand why the very mention of an Alliance meeting made the Hawthorne alpha's eye twitch.

"I'm sure you had nothing to do with that decision," Daria told Melody sharply.

"Why, I'm hurt you'd suggest such a thing, Daria." The fae's laugh tinkled like wind chimes in a hurricane guaranteed to level your house.

I finally clocked what it was about her that had intrigued my wolf.

Melody carried the scent of magic too.

I was busy trying to figure out how that was possible when a noise at the far end of the table drew my gaze. A dwarf with an impressive braided beard and arms that looked like they could bench-press a small car sat on a high chair. His scent was earthy and metallic.

He also stank of alcohol.

"Finnic Ironfall," Victoria said in a low voice. "He speaks for the dwarf clans."

Finnic caught me looking and raised a tankard that had definitely not been provided by the Chamber of Commerce.

"To the white wolf," he boomed, cheeks flushed and eyes gleaming. "May your enemies flee before you like rabbits before the hunt!"

"Er, thank you?" I said uncertainly in the frosty silence.

A delicate-looking woman with gossamer wings that shimmered faintly in the conference room lighting rolled her eyes next to the dwarf.

"I'm Titania Rohentyn, pixie representative," she said in a voice like silver bells. "Ignore Finnic. He's been celebrating since noon."

"Celebrating what?" Bo whispered curiously under the table.

I hushed him.

Finnic overheard my dog. "Friday," the dwarf said proudly.

Faint grumbles broke around the table. From the snatches I caught, it appeared Finnic always had something to celebrate at the Alliance meetings.

A man who looked like he could be Gavin's much more serious older brother drummed his fingers irritably on the table.

"Perhaps we could maintain some semblance of decorum?" His nostrils sparked slightly as he spoke. "We *are* Alliance members, after all." He caught my stare. "I'm Wendall Baird, the representative for the dragon newt coalition," he confessed gruffly.

I chewed my lip. "Coalition" sounded very official.

Wendall looked like he'd read my mind.

"We take our civic duties seriously," the dragon newt stated with an austere dignity that suggested he'd never accidentally set fire to important paperwork, unlike another dragon newt I knew and associated with regularly.

The last figure at the table was partially hidden in the shadows. This seemed to be either a lighting problem or a deliberate aesthetic choice. I caught a glimpse of pale skin and sharp cheekbones belonging to someone who looked like he'd embraced the concept of brooding since birth.

The trace of sulfur that danced across my nostrils told me he was a demon.

"Oscar Roosevelt," he said in a voice like silk over steel. "I represent the independent supernatural community."

"That's a fancy way of saying 'miscellaneous monsters,'" Titania explained helpfully.

Daria cleared her throat. The ambient chatter around the table died down.

"Now that introductions have been made, let's bring this meeting to order," the witch said in a businesslike voice. "We have several items on tonight's agenda, but I believe we should begin with the most pressing matter. The disposition of the crystal skull recovered from the recent…incident."

All eyes turned to me. I resisted the urge to sink into my chair.

"The artifact is currently secured in our containment facility," Daria continued, consulting her notes. "However, the question remains as to its ultimate fate."

"We should destroy it, of course," Wendall said immediately. "Nothing good ever comes from objects of that magnitude of dark power."

"Spoken like someone who's never had to deal with magical artifact disposal," Gregory said with a frown. "You can't simply throw something like that in a furnace, Wendall. The magical backlash could level half the town."

"Then what do you suggest?" Cornelius asked thinly.

"We should study it," Oscar declared portentously from his shadowy corner of Hell. "This is a once-in-a-lifetime opportunity to learn from a cursed artifact. Knowledge is power, after all."

Melody looked like she was in agreement with the demon.

I, on the other hand, didn't like the sound of that one bit.

Finnic's words echoed my thoughts.

"Knowledge is also how you accidentally do something stupid," the dwarf groused, taking another swig from his tankard. "I speak from experience."

"The point remains, we need to decide what to do with the skull," Daria said firmly.

Pearl surprised everyone by jumping on the table.

She waited until she had everyone's undivided attention before dropping a bombshell.

"Might I suggest that since the Hawthorne luna was the one to neutralize the artifact's power, her opinion should carry significant weight in this decision?"

# DECISIONS AND DISTRACTIONS

THE SILENCE THAT FOLLOWED PEARL'S PRONOUNCEMENT was so thick you could have cut it with a silver knife and served it at a vampire dinner party.

Victoria and Samuel were staring at Pearl like she'd lost her feline mind.

"Pearl?" the Hawthorne matriarch said uneasily.

"*What are doing?!*" Samuel hissed at the cat. "We said we wouldn't let Abby get involved in Alliance matters!"

"*You* said you wouldn't let Abby get involved in Alliance matters," Pearl retorted. "I know you want to protect your luna, but it's pretty clear she needs to step up if we want to stop the Alliance from doing something stupid, like the dwarf says."

"Hear, hear," Finnic said, waving his tankard unhelpfully.

Every pair of eyes in the room had swiveled to me with an intensity that made me want to crawl under the table. Which, considering the table was occupied by some of the most powerful supernatural creatures on the East Coast, probably wouldn't have helped anyway.

"Well," Daria said slowly, her pen hovering over her notepad. She put it down and leaned back in her chair. "That's a novel perspective." She fixed me with a penetrating stare. "Even though Abby is not officially an Alliance member, I think we should hear her thoughts on the matter."

"The white wolf did demonstrate considerable influence over the artifact," Cornelius agreed with a grunt. "She's probably the only one who can control it without tapping into a ley line."

I bit my lip worriedly. It was clear from the Tremaines's and Portia's anxious expressions that they were thinking about how the white wolf had commanded an entire ballroom full of supernatural elites to sit down like obedient puppies.

Wendall's nostrils sparked again. "With respect to Ms. West's unique abilities, this is hardly her area of expertise." His tone suggested he was finding this whole situation about as appealing as a root canal performed by a troll.

"Neither is it yours, Wendall," Melody pointed out with that dangerously sweet smile of hers. "When was the last time any of us dealt with a cursed artifact of this magnitude?"

"The 1800s," Gregory muttered under his breath.

"Exactly my point," the witch-fae continued blithely. "We're all flying blind here. At least Abby has actually used the thing."

I shifted uncomfortably in my chair. I wasn't sure

"used" was the right word. It had been more like desperate improvisation spurred on by my wolf. I said as much.

"That's the best kind of improv," Finnic declared, raising his tankard again. "Nothing teaches you about magic quite like nearly dying from it." His eyes hardened a little. "Ask me how I know."

I was starting to get the feeling the dwarf had either led an especially dangerous life or was as accident prone as my best friend Ellie.

Samuel leaned forward stiffly, his protective instincts humming through our bond. "Abby's connection to the skull was circumstantial. She was trying to save lives, not conduct a magical experiment."

No one missed the slight growl underscoring his voice.

"Nevertheless," Oscar said from his arena of darkness, "the fact remains that she succeeded where others would have failed. That suggests a natural affinity that shouldn't be dismissed." His gimlet eyes studied me like a cat would a mouse it had found wandering inside its food bowl.

"Or it suggests she got lucky," Wendall shot back.

I was about to express heartfelt agreement with the dragon newt when Samuel spoke.

"Lucky?" An edge had crept into his voice. "You think it was *luck* that let my luna stop an entire ballroom full of supernatural creatures from tearing each other apart?"

Victoria's expression turned glassy. "Samuel, you're meant to be downplaying Abby's role in that incident."

Samuel looked like he was past caring at this point.

I had to admit, my alpha coming to my defense made my insides all warm and gooey. Of course, that could also be acid.

The dragon newt had the grace to look slightly abashed at Samuel's glower. "I merely meant—"

"You meant that because she's new to our world, she couldn't possibly understand the complexities of magical artifacts," Samuel interrupted. "Sometimes an outsider's perspective is exactly what we need, though." He scanned the table, his expression stony. "Everyone in that ballroom was so busy following the rules of engagement they'd established over centuries that they couldn't see the forest for the trees. Had it not been for Abby, we'd all be slaves pandering to Camilla's every whim right now."

A heavy silence fell over the room. Daria broke it.

"Which brings us back to my original question," the witch said succinctly. "What are we going to do about it?"

I became the object of everyone's stares and realized they wanted an answer from me.

"Sometimes the best solution is the simplest one," I said hesitantly.

"And what would that be?" Daria asked.

"Lock it away. Somewhere secure. Preferably heavily warded, so it can't hurt anyone ever again." I paused. "And then everyone should do their best to forget it even exists."

The Alliance exchanged wary glances.

"That's asking a lot from a bunch of supernatural

creatures who like to dream up ways of stabbing each other in the back," Cornelius said with a heavy sigh.

"Exactly," Oscar added with a surly pout from his alcove of gloom.

"It's a good thing we have a white luna in town," Portia said sharply.

Melody ignored her fellow Alliance members and studied me with otherworldly eyes. "You don't want to understand how it works? How you were able to channel its power?"

"Nope," I said firmly. "Holding that thing was the spookiest thing I've ever done in my life." I made a face. "Never mind the naked guy that popped out of nowhere straight after."

Samuel, Victoria, Portia, and the Tremaines shuddered at the memory of a nude Arthur Holt. Pearl looked like she was considering regurgitating a fur ball.

Daria cleared her throat and rapped the table with a gavel. "Alright. All those in favor of securing the crystal skull in our containment facility indefinitely?"

Hands went up around the table. Victoria, Samuel, Gregory, Constantia, Wendall, Cornelius, Portia, Finnic, and somewhat reluctantly, Titania.

"Opposed?"

Oscar raised his hand. Melody hesitated, then did the same.

"Abstaining?" Daria asked distractedly for the sake of it while she made notes.

Bo put his paw up. Everyone stared at him, Pearl with a heavy dose of pity.

"You're not a member of the Alliance," Daria pointed out coolly.

Bo wagged his tail. "I was trying to lighten the heavy atmosphere."

Daria's face took on the expression of someone who'd spent far too long in my dog's company. "Motion carries. The skull will remain in our containment facility." She glanced at me. "Thank you for your input, Abby. It was illuminating."

I wasn't sure if that was a compliment or a polite way of saying I'd confirmed everyone's worst fears about letting newbies into Alliance meetings.

"Right, then." Daria consulted her agenda. "Next item. Gregory, I believe you have some concerns about recent activities in your territory?"

"Yes. There have been some minor incidents at several of the blood banks in the area. Small amounts of inventory have gone missing."

"How small?" Wendall asked.

"A few pints here and there. Nothing that would suggest organized theft, but enough to be noticed."

Finnic waved dismissively. "It's probably just a hungry fledgling who hasn't learned proper vampire etiquette yet."

Cornelius and Titania nodded.

I debated asking how one became a vampire fledging and where blood banks got their blood from but decided to file those questions in my things-I-should-never-ask folder. I pursed my lips.

Judging from recent episodes, this folder should

also include never asking supernatural creatures about their lineage, diet, or personal sanitation.

"That was my first thought as well," Gregory said with a faint frown. "However, the pattern is unusual. The thefts are happening during daylight hours, which suggests either a very bold fledgling or something else entirely."

"Could be a ghoul," Melody suggested. "They're not bound by the same limitations as vampires."

"Or a human who's discovered our community," Oscar added ominously from his belt of gloominess.

"We're investigating all possibilities," Gregory said. "We simply wanted to make the Alliance aware of the situation in case anyone knew something that could help us find who's behind it."

"Thank you, Gregory." Daria looked around the table. "Anything else pressing? Or shall we call it a night?" she said with undisguised hope.

"Actually," Melody said, her voice taking on a dangerous sing-song quality that even I was starting to recognize as meaning trouble, "I wanted to discuss the upcoming winter solstice celebrations. There have been some territorial disputes regarding venue assignments."

The temperature in the room dropped several degrees.

It was clear the term "territorial dispute" was a red flag in the Alliance's world.

I recalled that one of Hawthorne & Associates's roles was to manage said disputes and shot a wary look at Samuel.

My alpha's eyes had darkened. "What kind of territorial disputes?"

"Oh, nothing too serious," Melody said in a tone that made it clear it was in fact deadly serious. "Just the usual disagreements about who gets to use the old cemetery for their rituals. And possibly some hexing. Very minor hexing, really." She laughed.

The temperature in the room was now rapidly approaching subzero.

"Define 'minor,'" Samuel said flatly.

"Well, nobody's been turned into a toad. Permanently, I mean."

I caught Victoria's eye. Her expression mirrored my own thoughts about the many different ways this situation could go catastrophically wrong and how badly Samuel was going to react to it. I swallowed a sigh.

And here everyone was worried about how *I* was going to behave at this meeting.

Bo chose that moment to stick his head up above the table. "Are we almost done? Because I need to pee and I'd hate to do it here, with all of you watching. No offense, but some of you really creep me out."

The Alliance members stared at my dog, nonplussed. A few faintly accusing gazes switched to me.

"It's not like I can control his mouth," I said guiltily.

A handful of frowns suggested I should.

"Right," Daria said, rubbing her temple. "Perhaps we should table the solstice discussions for now and reconvene next week to address the territorial disputes."

"Probably for the best," Cornelius agreed. "These things tend to sort themselves out if you give them time."

"Or explode spectacularly," Titania added blithely.

Samuel groaned.

"Thank you for that optimistic assessment," Wendall muttered.

"Motion to adjourn?" Gregory suggested.

"Seconded," came from multiple voices around the table.

"All in favor?" Daria asked.

Every hand shot up with suspicious speed.

"Meeting adjourned," Daria announced, relieved. "Same time next week, assuming we all survive the interim."

The Alliance members nodded at me curtly as they started filing out of the room. I couldn't help but notice the way they gave me a wide berth.

"Well, that could have gone worse," I said. "At least I didn't offend anyone."

"Oh, you did, dear," Victoria murmured.

"I did?" I stared. "But—everyone was being nice. And the building is still standing."

Samuel, Victoria, and Pearl exchanged a look.

"What?" I asked suspiciously.

"You were doing that thing you did at the ball," Samuel explained quietly.

I blinked. "What thing?" I froze, my belly clenching as I grasped their meaning. "Wait. You don't mean that white wolf pacifier thing where I unconsciously soothe supernatural creatures' emotions?!"

"Yes," Samuel confirmed stiffly. He faltered. "I don't think any of them realized it was happening."

My stomach sank. "And if they had?"

"We'd be scraping bits of you off the burning wall right now," Pearl said with zero compunction.

Bo's ears flattened.

That answer was going to keep me up at night.

"If Elizabeth possessed such a power, it was never recorded anywhere," Victoria said in a troubled voice as we left the conference room. "We should try and figure out what it is."

Elizabeth Rochester Hawthorne was Victoria's great-great-grandmother and had been a white luna. Not only had she united the New England packs during the Shadow War that had coincided with the American Civil War, she was also responsible for creating the town of Amberford and several other supernatural settlements in New England.

"Maybe some things are better left as mysteries," Samuel suggested.

For once, I had to agree. The way my wolf had gone quiet told me we might regret finding out what that power was.

# 4

# BAD BLOOD AND BRAIN MUFFINS

I SPENT THE WEEKEND DODGING QUESTIONS FROM ELLIE about the Alliance meeting. Luckily, it didn't take much to distract my best friend.

Sunday morning was pack brunch at the Hawthornes and I found myself the unwelcome topic of conversation once again. It was a good thing I was too mellow after an intense night of passion involving my alpha and some bed posts to take offense at the wild suggestions flying around the table. James kept asking Samuel why he looked tired, Pearl made several scathing remarks about alpha stamina training, and Victoria was asking Bernard for a Bloody Mary by ten o'clock.

All in all, it was a standard Hawthorne family meeting.

"How did it go?" Charlene said the moment Bo and I stepped into the lobby of Hawthorne & Associates on Monday.

Fred materialized from the room behind the

reception desk with the kind of speed that suggested he'd been lurking there just waiting for us to arrive.

"Did anyone try to kill you?"

I sighed at the half demon's bloodthirsty tone. I didn't even have to ask what they were talking about. Chances were, someone in the building had a betting pool going about my fate on Friday night.

"Really? That's the first thing you guys want to ask?"

"It's a legitimate question," Fred said defensively. "Alliance meetings have a reputation, after all."

"He's not wrong," Bo huffed. "Those people were weird."

No one pointed out that a sassy, talking Husky of indeterminate supernatural lineage was even weirder.

"Remember what happened when the gargoyles tried to join?" Charlene reminded Fred worriedly. "Half of downtown had to be rebuilt."

"The gargoyles tried to join the Alliance?" I asked warily.

"Maybe we shouldn't talk about the gargoyle incident." Fred looked over his shoulder and shuddered.

I made a mental note to ask Samuel about the gargoyle incident later. Assuming I survived whatever fresh hell this day was about to throw at me. Three weeks working for Hawthorne & Associates had taught me one thing if nothing else.

Okay, two.

My coworkers were batshit crazy. And the supernatural community of Amberford was even more so.

"But seriously," Charlene said in a voice that was half zeal and half dread, "how was your first meeting? Did Daria try to hex anyone? Did the dragon newt set anything on fire?" She paused and gulped. "Please tell me Finnic didn't bring his drinking horn, get totally wasted, and throw his axe at someone?"

Bo and I exchanged an uneasy glance. It seemed Friday's meeting had been exceedingly mild compared to usual standards.

"He brought a tankard," I admitted, seeing the dwarf chieftain in a whole new light.

Charlene and Fred traded knowing looks.

Bo and I took the elevator to the fifth floor.

Janet, Gavin, Didi, Mindy, and even Nigel were loitering in the open office area in a suspicious cluster. Bo and I became the object of intense stares once more.

"Oh, hey, Abby," Janet said with forced casualness. "We were just thinking of having a coffee break. Want to join us?"

I looked at the clock on the wall and frowned. "Isn't it too early for a coffee break?"

"The early bird gets the supernatural politics gossip," Didi declared with unashamed honesty.

"You might as well give up and spill the beans," Bo told me stoically. "These guys are like a dog with a bone when they want answers. I should know."

Mindy abandoned any pretense of subtlety and flickered into full visibility. "Did you accidentally command anyone to do anything embarrassing? Did the dog insult someone important?" She leaned forward excitedly. "Did you threaten to punch anybody?!"

I narrowed my eyes. "Why does everyone assume I threatened to punch someone?"

"Pattern recognition," Gavin said promptly.

"They're not wrong," Bo panted, tail swinging.

I scowled. I could hardly deny their inference.

"For the record," I said with as much dignity as I could muster, "I did not threaten to punch anyone at the Alliance meeting."

The others looked crestfallen at this news.

"How disappointingly mature of you," Didi muttered.

I was debating which one of them to punch when Hugh appeared around the corner. He slowed at our sight.

"I see word has gotten out about the meeting," Samuel's brother said with mild exasperation.

"Word got out the moment Abby left the building," Janet said. "Fred had a betting pool going on whether she would survive her first Alliance encounter."

My mouth pressed to a thin line.

Hugh saw my expression and hastily addressed the others.

"How about you people disband before Samuel catches you standing around gossiping?"

A commotion from the direction of Samuel's office reached us right on cue. The group dispersed with supernatural speed, though several people lingered by their desks in obvious eavesdropping positions. Nigel developed a sudden fascination with the water cooler.

Samuel appeared, his expression grim enough to make the ambient temperature drop several degrees. My belly tightened.

Damn if I didn't find his grumpy look sexy.

He shot me a wary look and cleared his throat.

"Abby, Didi, Gavin. My office. Now."

Bo's tail drooped as we followed Didi and Gavin toward Samuel's office. "So much for a quiet morning."

I made a face. "When have we ever had a quiet morning in this place?"

Barney was making coffee in Samuel's office. His expression made it clear he didn't want to be there. My gaze landed on the open takeout box beside him.

Bo's ears flattened. "Are those brain muffins?"

"Yes," Barney said morosely. "They're fresh from Ghoul's Kitchen, on Fifth Street."

Bo slinked behind me.

"Barney," Didi said carefully, "why do you have brain muffins?"

"They were having a special. Buy five, get six free. Seemed wasteful not to take advantage." The vampire's tone turned even more glum. "Besides, it looks like I won't be able to get my usual blood fix for a while. This was the next best alternative."

My scalp prickled. I suddenly recalled Gregory's report at the Alliance meeting.

"Does that have anything to do with those blood bank thefts?"

Didi frowned. "What blood bank thefts?"

Barney and Samuel traded a loaded look.

"You'd better sit down," Samuel said.

Ten minutes later I began wondering whether my life had peaked at "accidentally turned into a werewolf" and everything since then had been a steady decline into "how is this my actual existence?"

Because I was currently drinking vampire-made coffee that could strip paint while listening to my alpha explain to me, Didi, and Gavin why someone robbing a blood bank on Saturday night was now apparently our problem.

Samuel ignored our sullen expressions and slid a file across the table. "Whoever did this almost cleaned out the facility, including the products in the emergency reserves. The Tremaines want us to investigate."

Didi, Gavin, and I looked at the folder like it had cooties.

"Weren't Gregory and Constantia already looking into the thefts?" I hazarded with thinly veiled hope.

"They were," Samuel confirmed. "This is too big an incident for them to handle on their own."

The witch and the dragon newt gave me "you open it" looks. I nearly pointed out they had seniority over me but decided this would be a waste of my breath.

I pulled the file over and opened it gingerly.

Bo peered over my arm, his eyes alive with the ghoulish interest of a dog obsessed with true crime shows.

"When you say 'cleaned out,' you mean someone stole the blood products, right? Not that they, er, consumed everything on site?" I said as I cautiously studied the crime scene photos of the empty blood bank.

To my relief and Bo's disappointment, there was a glaring lack of bodies and gratuitous gore. I passed the file to Didi and Gavin.

"Stole," Barney confirmed. "We think whoever did this is an expert."

I arched an eyebrow. "Vampire?"

"More than likely. Hence why Samuel wants me to join your team for this investigation."

I hesitated. Barney was Hawthorne & Associates's Head of Finance and Investments. That seemed a far cry from vampire detective.

"Barney has experience in the field," Samuel grunted, no doubt picking up my unease through our bond.

Gavin's morning coffee steamed faintly from his nostrils. "Do we have any security footage from the bank?"

"Only a partial recording." Samuel worked his keyboard and showed us his computer screen. "The ghouls who run the place said the perpetrator took the cameras offline shortly after this. They still don't know how. He locked the night staff in a closet."

Didi, Gavin, and I studied the short, blurry black-and-white video.

It depicted a tall figure in Victorian-era clothing moving faster than the cameras could track in the lobby of the blood bank.

"So we're looking for a really old vampire with questionable fashion sense?" I said with a grimace.

Didi curled a lip. "Please. All vampires have questionable fashion sense." She shot a pointed look at the elbow patches on Barney's suit.

Barney bristled. "I'll have you know that this suit cost an arm and a leg!"

Bo brightened. "Whose?"

Samuel's mouth twitched.

Barney narrowed his eyes at my dog. "What's his blood group again?"

Bo's tail drooped.

"Anything else we need to know?" I said hastily while my dog quietly crawled under my chair.

"Yes." Samuel's expression turned sour. "The thief also broke into the administrative offices and stole some medical records."

"Anyone we know?" Didi asked.

"Only the most powerful vampires in the region," Samuel grunted.

Gavin's tail popped out. "That's not good."

"No, it isn't." Samuel sighed and ran a hand through his hair. "I don't even want to think about what the thief intends to do with them."

I raised a hand hesitantly. "Aren't medical records digital these days?"

Samuel, Didi, Barney, and Gavin gave me pitying looks.

"What?" I asked defensively.

"Vampires and ghouls are leery of new technologies," Samuel explained. "They keep paper copies of everything."

I suddenly remembered Barney's vintage typewriter and his two-finger typist attitude.

The vampire rapped said fingers on his armrest, his expression troubled. "Those medical records were pretty extensive. They contained the genealogical files for every major vampire bloodline in New England."

That got my attention. "Genealogical files?"

"Family trees, lineage documentation," the vampire explained with a wave of a hand. "The kind of information that would be invaluable to someone planning something nefarious."

I swallowed a sigh. Chasing after supernatural creatures doing nefarious things sounded about as fun as tap dancing across a lava pit in flip-flops.

Gavin's horns smoked slightly. "Could it be someone with an academic interest in vampire genetics?"

"I doubt it," Samuel said curtly. "Worst-case scenario, they intend to use this data to target those specific bloodlines. For what reason, we still don't know." He met our gazes steadily. "That's what you're going to find out."

I studied the security footage still on the screen.

"So where is this blood bank?" I said with as much enthusiasm as I could muster, which was hardly any.

# 5

# BANKING ON TROUBLE

ETERNAL RESERVES OCCUPIED A CONVERTED VICTORIAN mansion in the Crossroads. The building squatted between a twenty-four-hour laundromat and a taxidermy shop. The sign in the latter's window advertised *Undead Pet Preservation Services*, which I wisely decided not to ask anyone about.

The only hints that this wasn't your average blood bank were the tinted windows and the discreet brass nameplate that read *Specialized Supernatural Medical Storage Facility*.

"Subtle," I muttered as we climbed the front steps.

"Vampires aren't known for their marketing skills," Didi observed.

"This is actually an improvement," Gavin said. "The last blood bank I visited with a vampire friend had a neon sign that said *Type O and Go*."

Barney had the grace to look embarrassed at his brethren's lack of tact.

Bo slowed warily as we approached the front door.

"This place smells like a hospital had a baby with a butcher shop."

The Husky wasn't wrong. My skin fairly itched and my wolf wanted to bare her fangs at the scent of blood wafting from the building.

"By the way, where do blood banks get their blood from?" I asked distractedly.

"From other supernatural creatures," Barney replied. "And vampires."

That made me pause. "Vampires drink other vampires' blood?"

"Isn't that like, cannibalism?" Bo asked warily.

"You try to eat your tail on a regular basis," Barney reminded the Husky coolly.

"Some humans like to donate blood as well," Didi volunteered while Bo huffed indignantly. "The ones who know of Amberford's supernatural side." She shrugged at my stare. "Humans have weird fetishes."

The interior of Eternal Reserves was all sterile white walls, clinical lighting, and an eye-watering aroma of antiseptic that failed to mask the blood smell. The furniture was garishly cheerful and had evidently been chosen to make people forget that the place was basically a supernatural deli.

A woman with gray skin looked up from behind a desk as we entered. Her smile was bright enough to power a small city.

"Welcome to Eternal Reserves," she said with disarming enthusiasm. "Are you here for a deposit? I'm afraid we're not doing withdrawals right now. Just so you know, we're especially in need of O-negative."

"We're with Hawthorne & Associates." Didi showed the woman her ID. "We're here about the break-in."

The woman's smile faded until it could barely illuminate a medium-sized village.

"Ah. We've been expecting you. I'm Gladys Flintbone, the facility manager." She came around the desk. "Would you like some refreshments while we talk? I just made fresh brain muffins."

"That's very kind, but—" I started glassily.

"Oh, don't worry," Gladys interrupted. "They're gluten-free. And they're made with only the finest organic ingredients. Well, mostly organic. The brains are locally sourced. Ha-ha."

"Ha-ha," I echoed leadenly.

Bo tucked his tail firmly between his legs.

"We're fine, thank you," Didi stated firmly.

Gladys looked disappointed. "Are you sure?" She brightened a little. "I also have some lovely finger sandwiches. Actual finger sandwiches, not the boring kind humans make."

"We wouldn't say no to coffee," Gavin suggested.

"You've already had coffee this morning," Didi told the dragon newt.

Gavin's horns popped out. "I can have a second cup," he said with a hefty dose of belligerence.

Didi and I traded a look. One thing I'd come to learn in the last three weeks was that an over-caffeinated Gavin was a dangerous Gavin.

"Perhaps we could speak with whoever was on duty on Saturday night?" Barney said coolly.

Gladys blinked. "Oh. Mr. Bludworth. I didn't see you there."

I was wondering how anyone could ignore a skulking, six-foot-tall vampire who smelled faintly of mothballs when I realized he was doing his "fading into the background" vampire thing again, which took me by surprise the first time he did it at the office a week ago. So much so I inadvertently screamed the place down. This caused everyone to rush over, including a multi-eyed and tentacled Nigel who'd forgotten to adopt his human form in the heat of the moment. Which resulted in even more inadvertent screaming.

"Follow me," Gladys said. "I'll get everyone in the break room."

She led us down a hallway lined with decorative medical equipment displays that looked like they'd originated from the medieval ages.

The break room was a mix of normal office furniture and items that didn't look like standard corporate issue. A microwave sat next to what appeared to be a small crematorium. A coffee maker shared counter space with several glass containers full of things I didn't want to identify. A rack of brain muffins was cooling next to an industrial-sized oven that could easily house several children.

"Are you sure I can't tempt you with—?" Gladys started, gesturing toward the baked goods.

"No," Didi, Gavin, Bo, and I said as one.

"I'll try one," Barney volunteered.

Gladys beamed, took a china plate from a cupboard, and served him a muffin with reverence.

Barney bit into it. His eyes widened a little. "This is nice."

"The secret is in the marinade," Gladys said proudly. "Most people just throw the brains in raw, but I like to let them soak in a nice wine reduction first."

My eyes glazed over a little.

Barney met our faintly accusing stares as Gladys left the room in search of her coworkers.

"It would have been rude to refuse," he said defensively. "Ghouls are very proud of their cooking." He tucked into the rest of his muffin with obvious gusto.

"Right," Gavin muttered.

"This guy just likes brain muffins," Bo whispered accusingly.

Gladys returned with three ghouls.

They all had matching gray skin and name tags that read *Hi! I'm Dead, How Can I Help You?*

"This is Pete, Bethany, and Steve," Gladys introduced. "They were all here on the night of the robbery."

Pete waved shyly. His left arm dropped off.

Bethany picked it up and reattached it without a word.

"Let me make you that coffee." Gladys busied herself at the counter while we sat at a round table that had seen better centuries. "What would you like? We have regular, decaf, and plasma blend."

"Regular, please," I said quickly. Didi and Gavin murmured the same.

"Plasma blend," came Barney's unsurprising answer.

Gladys looked at Bo.

"He doesn't do coffee," I said.

Bo wagged his tail. "I had it once and I don't remember the next five hours of my life," he said with misplaced pride.

"He ran around the park like he was possessed," I said at Didi's and Gavin's questioning looks.

Steve, who seemed to be the most intact of the ghouls, spoke. "It's terrible about the break-in." He shook his head sadly.

Bo stared with bated breath and looked a little disappointed when Steve's head didn't fall off.

"We take security very seriously here," Pete added. "Well, we did. Now we're thinking of getting one of those fancy alarm systems."

"About time," Bethany muttered. "The taxidermist next door has more security tech than we do."

Gladys served us our drinks before taking a seat at the table. "Now, then, what would you like to know?"

Didi pulled out her notepad and clicked her pen with a sound like someone cocking a gun.

"Can you walk us through what happened that night?"

Pete, Bethany, and Steve exchanged wary looks.

"It was around midnight," Pete began. "It was my turn in the security room. I noticed the cameras going dark. At first I thought it was just a power glitch. Happens all the time in these old buildings." He waved a hand vaguely at the ceiling.

Bethany caught it with lightning-fast speed as it dropped off his wrist.

Bo started wagging his tail.

I eyed my dog's keen eyes suspiciously. I sure as hell hoped he wasn't thinking of treating one of Pete's body parts like a fetching stick.

"Sorry." Pete twisted his hand back on with an embarrassed expression.

"No problem," Gavin hummed.

I looked around at his tone and swallowed a groan.

The dragon newt's horns were now fully visible and his pupils were dilated.

Didi cursed and yanked his cup out of his hands.

"Hey!" the dragon newt protested. "I was drinking that."

"And now you're not, so zip it," Didi hissed.

A headache started thrumming at my temples.

"What happened after that?" I asked the ghouls, pretending not to notice Gavin's heavily smoking nostrils.

"The temperature dropped," Steve said.

I stared. "The temperature dropped?"

Steve nodded. "Yes. Really dropped. Like, morgue-cold dropped."

Barney leaned forward, pupils gleaming crimson for a worrying second.

"Did you see the intruder?" the vampire asked sharply.

"We caught a glimpse of him before he locked us up," Bethany said. "He was tall, very pale. Dressed like he was heading to a nineteenth-century costume party."

"What about his face?" I asked. "Could you pick him out of a lineup?"

"No." Pete grimaced. "He moved so fast everything looked blurry."

"Did he say anything?" Barney pressed.

Pete, Bethany, and Steve exchanged a glance.

"Not to us," Steve said reluctantly. "But we did hear him humming while he was clearing out the place."

# 6

# COFFEE, MISTAKES, AND ALIBIS

THAT GOT EVERYONE'S ATTENTION.

"Humming?" I repeated.

"Classical music," Pete said, nodding. His head slipped slightly to the left.

"Beautiful melody," Steve admitted. "Very haunting."

Barney had gone very still. "What piece?"

I could practically feel the tension vibrating off the vampire.

"I'm afraid I don't recall the name," Steve said apologetically. "But it was lovely. Very dramatic. Had this famous singing bit at the end."

Barney flinched. "Beethoven's Ninth Symphony?"

"That's the one!" Steve beamed.

Didi flashed a small frown at Barney before focusing on the ghouls. "How long was the perp here?"

"Couldn't have been more than fifteen minutes." Bethany shrugged. "He was very efficient. Like he knew exactly what he wanted and where to find it."

My scalp prickled. It seemed Samuel and Barney had been right.

This thief was no amateur.

"How did you get out of the closet?" I asked curiously.

The look the ghouls exchanged made me regret the question.

"Pete detached an arm and sent it inside the vent to unlock the door from outside," Steve said.

"We can control our body parts remotely," Bethany explained at my expression.

Yup, that was going to give me nightmares.

Didi finished taking notes and looked up from her notepad. "Who was the last customer who visited the blood bank that day?"

Confusion washed across Gladys's face. "Why do you want to know that?"

"Because it might be relevant to our investigation."

Steve hesitated. "It was that nice young man who comes in every week. Very polite. He always asks about our specials."

"His name is Virgil," Bethany elaborated. "He works at that coffee shop in Sycamore Grove."

My mouth went dry. "You mean Virgil from Bean Me Up?!"

"Yes," Steve confirmed. "He was here right before closing time."

"What did he do?" I asked, desperately trying to keep my tone casual.

"He just got his regular order," Bethany said. "Type A negative, two pints. He made a deposit for payment."

I blinked. "Deposit? You mean, he donated blood?"

"Yes," Pete said. "The Tremaine reserve is particularly popular."

You could have heard a pin drop in the hush that followed.

"Tremaine?" I repeated dully.

Didi's eyes rounded. "Wait. You mean, like Gregory and Constantia Tremaine?!"

"Ho boy," Bo huffed excitedly.

Pete looked horrified at his faux pas. He attempted to cover his mouth with his hand. His arm fell off. He picked up the limb and covered his eyes with it instead.

Barney sighed and pinched the bridge of his nose. "Gregory is going to lose his mind."

"Yup," Gavin agreed with a sickly expression.

"Barney knowing is one thing, but you knew too?!" Didi asked the dragon newt accusingly.

"Virgil and I went to the same school," Gavin said defensively. "Also, his true identity is meant to be a secret."

Gladys had gone deathly pale.

"You know our clients' information is confidential, Pete," she croaked.

"I know," Pete mumbled while Bethany and Steve patted his back sympathetically and helped him reattach his limb. "I'm sorry. I crumbled under the pressure of the interrogation."

Ghouls were nowhere near as scary as I thought they'd be. Bar their unhealthy obsession with brain muffins, they were actually pretty nice.

I finally recovered from the shocking revelation

that Bean Me Up's vampire barista was somehow connected to the Tremaines. "Did Virgil act funny in any way while he was here?"

"Not really," Steve said.

"He looked distracted," Bethany contributed. "And he kept looking at our client board."

I stared. "Client board?"

Bethany left the room and returned with a clipboard that looked like a wine cellar inventory. Instead of vintages, it listed blood types and donors.

"We like to let our customers know the options we have available, so we keep these lists in the withdrawal rooms," Gladys explained at my pinched look.

The pieces were starting to form a picture I didn't like.

Virgil being at the blood bank the night it was robbed and being related to the Tremaines weren't the only things I was concerned about.

Ellie was working at Bean Me Up and Virgil was her boss.

"We'll need a record of everything that was taken," Barney said in a hard voice.

We left Eternal Reserves and made our way across town to Sycamore Grove.

Bean Me Up looked the same as it had three weeks ago, when I'd first stumbled across Amberford's supernatural community. The only difference was that there were more macramé plants and crystals in the windows and someone had added the words *and Clean Fun!* to the board sign on the sidewalk that said *Ethically Sourced Coffee and Good Vibes.*

I recognized Ellie's handwriting.

"Do you think she'll make me one of those dog-friendly drinks she always talks about?" Bo said in a voice full of hope as we approached the entrance.

"You know what happened the last time you had coffee, right?" I reminded him.

"Technically, I don't have any recollection of that incident," my dog sassed. "Also, that was human coffee. This is supernatural coffee."

"I hardly think that's going to be any better."

The bell above the door jingled when Gavin pushed it open.

The interior was busier than I remembered, the usual mix of supernatural creatures and oblivious humans scattered across the vintage tables and chairs of the café in a pre-lunch rush.

Ellie spotted us from behind the counter. She beamed and waved enthusiastically, nearly knocking over a stack of cups in the process. Though she looked frazzled and sported what appeared to be coffee stains in her hair, my best friend looked happy.

"Perfect timing," she said excitedly as I approached. "I was just about to make a new batch of —" She stopped mid-sentence when she noticed Didi, Gavin, and Barney behind me. Her smile faded a little. "Oh. Hi. Are you here for the, um, special drinks?"

I noticed Bo staring at a couple of the tables.

The vampires sitting there looked tired. Not just tired, but drained, like they hadn't fed properly in days.

Barney frowned at them faintly.

"Actually, we're here on business," Didi told Ellie. "Is Virgil around?"

"He's in the back doing inventory," Ellie said uncertainly. "Do you want me to get him?"

Gavin's nostrils smoked a little as he stared at my best friend.

It seemed Ellie was going to be popular in both the human and supernatural world.

"We'd like to speak with Virgil, if that's okay," I told Ellie.

"Sure." Ellie turned toward the espresso machine and promptly knocked over a pitcher of what looked like red-tinted milk. "Oops." She grimaced. "Sorry, that's our special strawberry blend."

I watched my best friend clean up the spill and saw several vampire customers shudder out of the corner of my eye. A terrible suspicion began to form in my mind.

"Ellie," I said carefully, "how long have you been making the drinks on your own?"

"Oh, about a week now." She straightened and gave me a proud smile. "Virgil said he wanted to focus on the business side of things for a while, so he's been letting me handle most of the customer service. I'm getting really good at it. Well, mostly." She wrinkled her nose at the coffee machine. "That thing is a bit temperamental."

She disappeared into the back room before I could ask more questions. My wolf picked up muffled conversation. Ellie returned with Virgil.

The vampire was sporting bohemian clothes and a

preoccupied expression. He looked as far removed from being the firstborn scion of the most powerful vampire clan in Amberford as a poodle was from a wolf.

"Hi," Virgil said with an affable service smile. "How can I help?" His gaze landed on Gavin. His eyes widened a little. "Gavin?!"

"Hey, Virgil," the dragon newt said awkwardly.

"What are you doing here?"

"I work for Hawthorne & Associates," Gavin confessed.

Confusion clouded Virgil's face.

"I'm afraid we're here on an official capacity," Didi said briskly, flashing her badge. "We'd like to ask you some questions about the blood bank robbery."

# THE PLOT THICKENS

Virgil blinked, nonplussed. "What blood bank robbery?"

Ellie was pretending to make coffee behind him and failing badly.

My wolf and I could tell Virgil wasn't acting.

"We understand you were at Eternal Reserves on Saturday," I said quietly. "Someone broke into the place and pretty much cleaned it out that night."

Ellie almost dropped a cup.

Virgil stiffened. The vampire's friendly smile faded. "And I'm a suspect? Just because I visited the place that day?"

A burst of crimson power rolled off the barista.

I startled, my wolf stirring under my skin. It was gone as quickly as it had appeared, leaving a fading haze in the air I suspected only supernatural creatures could see.

Judging from the way Barney narrowed his eyes, it wasn't a figment of my imagination.

"We're not saying you're a suspect," the older vampire told Virgil in a hard voice, his gaze holding a crimson glint of warning. "But you might have seen or smelled something that could help us identify the culprit."

Didi made a face at Barney. "Are you sure you want to write him off the suspect list?"

Barney indicated Virgil irritably. "Does he look like he goes around humming Beethoven's Ninth Symphony?"

Didi studied the vampire barista with pursed lips. "You have a point."

"He had two in his—" Bo started helpfully before I hastily muzzled him with my hand.

Ellie reappeared at Virgil's elbow. I stared at what she was carrying as she stepped out from behind the counter.

It was a tray of drinks that looked suspiciously like regular coffee with red coloring.

"Ellie, wait—" Virgil started, alarmed.

She'd already reached a table.

"Two Type-O lattes and a B-positive cappuccino," she announced cheerfully.

We stared as the vampires reluctantly accepted their order and took polite sips that couldn't completely hide their disappointment.

I hated being right.

"She's been giving vampires normal coffee?" I asked Virgil.

Barney sucked in air. Gavin's horns popped out.

Didi muttered something under her breath that didn't sound like a compliment.

"The customers are too polite to complain. Besides, it's not like regular coffee will kill them." Virgil sighed and ran a hand through his hair. "I thought she was getting the hang of the supernatural drink recipes, but apparently I wasn't clear enough. I should have kept a closer eye on her."

Having known Ellie since preschool, I could see how Virgil had fallen into the trap of thinking she could understand simple instructions without a map. I shuddered as I recalled the sandpit incident of 2002.

My best friend had flooded the sandbox with the garden hose in a mistaken attempt to cool everyone down during a blistering summer. This resulted in a quagmire that had trapped five children, two teaching assistants, and Gerald, the school's pet hamster. The fire department chief said he'd never seen anything like it, a statement Ellie had chosen to take as a compliment rather than a dire indictment of her burgeoning life skills. Mrs. Henderson, our teacher, had to take the week off to recuperate from the trauma. As for Gerald the Hamster, he was never quite the same afterward.

"Is what you said true?" Virgil said warily. "Someone cleaned out Eternal Reserves?"

"They even hit the emergency stock," Gavin confirmed.

"Ouch." Virgil rubbed his chin, a thoughtful frown wrinkling his brow. "I'm afraid I didn't sense anything unusual while I was there."

"The staff we interviewed told us you looked a little preoccupied that day," I said carefully.

"And you seemed oddly fixated on their client board," Didi added with a grudging trace of suspicion.

Virgil's expression grew shuttered.

"I was just seeing if they had enough Type A negative," he finally confessed. "The other blood banks seem to have almost run out. And I've been having some—family issues lately."

"You mean, with the Tremaines?" Didi asked.

Virgil stiffened. "How did you know that?" He shot an accusing look at Gavin.

The dragon newt put his hands up. "It wasn't me. One of the blood bank staff accidentally spilled the beans."

"Besides, I know who you are," Barney said irritably.

Virgil didn't look happy about any of this.

"If you must know, my father's been pressuring me to come back to the family," he said stiffly. "Since he's not above using underhanded tactics to get what he wants, I've been kinda on edge lately."

Barney studied him for a moment. "I have to admit I wouldn't put anything past Gregory Tremaine, but sabotaging a coffee shop seems a bit far-fetched."

"You don't know my father like I do," Virgil said darkly. "He's never forgiven me for rejecting my role in our family. In his mind, I'm bringing shame to the Tremaine name by serving coffee to the masses instead of ruling over them from some ivory tower."

An awkward silence followed. I started to feel sorry for the vampire.

"I'm afraid we still have to ask you this. Where were you at midnight on Saturday?"

"At home, playing D&D with some guys from Milwaukee," Virgil replied promptly.

Gavin blinked. "You mean, the Langhorne brothers?"

"Yes."

"You know them?" I asked Gavin.

The dragon newt nodded. "Their cousin went to our school."

Which meant Virgil was telling the truth, since he knew Gavin would be able to check his alibi.

A crash from behind the counter interrupted our conversation. Ellie was trying to operate the espresso machine and had succeeded in covering herself and half the counter in coffee. She shot a guilty glance at Virgil.

"I should probably help her before she accidentally poisons someone," the vampire barista said with a sigh.

"Good idea."

Six hours later found us back at Hawthorne & Associates.

"So let me get this straight," Samuel said, his voice carrying a controlled calm that probably preceded someone getting fired or possibly fed to something with teeth. "There have been more blood bank thefts, but no one bothered to report them because they were afraid of upsetting the Tremaines?"

Bar a side trip to Stake My Shake for lunch, we'd

spent the day visiting most of the blood banks across Amberford. The results had been depressingly consistent; there had been varying amounts of inventory going missing at most of them, plenty of nervous ghoul staff, and a collective case of selective amnesia when it came to filing official reports.

The tension thrumming through the mate bond from my alpha put my wolf's teeth on edge. This case was turning out to be bigger than any of us had anticipated.

"That's about the size of it," Didi confirmed. "Crimson Curations lost several pints of AB negative last month. Midnight Supply had their entire O-positive stock depleted over the course of three weeks. And don't get me started on what happened at Plasma Palace."

Samuel groaned. "What happened at Plasma Palace?"

"Someone kept breaking in and stealing exactly one pint at a time," Gavin admitted. He scratched a horn. "It took some time for the staff to connect the dots."

None of us felt the need to inform Samuel that the staff at Plasma Palace were not the smartest tools in the supernatural tool box. Barney had words with the manager before we'd left. The ghoul had lost a couple of limbs in distress.

Samuel sat back in his chair and pinched the bridge of his nose.

I noted the faint circles under his eyes with a degree of concern until I realized I was likely the cause of them. Damn my wolf and her libido.

"So, bar our clue about a vampire who dresses like he's from the Victorian era and hums Beethoven's Ninth Symphony, we have nothing?" my alpha grumbled.

"No," Barney muttered. "And we still have no idea why he wanted those genealogical files."

"Maybe he's into family trees?" Bo suggested, busy snarfing a muffin he'd unearthed from God knows where.

We all looked at him.

The Husky finished swallowing and licked his chops. "Someone could be mapping out vampire bloodlines and cherry-picking specific types of blood to steal."

"That actually makes horrifying sense," Barney said grudgingly.

I studied Bo with something approaching admiration. Sometimes, my dog acted like a true genius.

"Or maybe they're planning something real terrible," the Husky continued with significantly more enthusiasm. "Like, I don't know, wiping out all inferior vampire bloodlines." His tail thrummed the air with macabre zeal. "I saw a TV show like that once. It was cool!"

And sometimes, my dog just acted like an utter nutjob.

Samuel scowled. "How about we have less useless speculation and more concrete ideas?" There was a knock on the door. "Come in," he called out irritably.

Janet stuck her head in, her expression apologetic.

"Sorry to interrupt, but Charlene just rang. Gregory and Constantia Tremaine are in the building. They're asking to speak with you about the blood bank investigation."

A fraught hush fell over the room. Didi and Gavin looked like they'd just been told Victoria and Pearl were here for a visit. Barney curled a lip like he'd swallowed a worm. Bo scratched an ear before examining his tail with the kind of focused expression that said he was thinking about chasing it.

Yup, things could be about to spiral down the drain to Shitsville.

Samuel nodded curtly at Janet, oblivious to my glum thoughts. "Send them in."

Janet disappeared and returned moments later with the power couple. Gregory wore a suit that made him look like he'd stepped out of a boardroom where billion-dollar deals were being discussed over afternoon tea. Constantia's dress screamed money, while her moue indicated her growing horror at having to mingle with Amberford's riffraff.

"Abby," Gregory greeted me politely.

"Gregory," I murmured.

The vampire couple tensed a little at the sight of Barney.

"Barnabas," Constantia said steadily. "You're looking well."

"As are you, Constantia," Barney said in a formal tone that hinted at some past history.

Gregory's face tightened.

Definitely some drama there.

Samuel gestured to a couple of empty chairs. "Please, sit. I assume you're here about the break-in at Eternal Reserves?"

"Among other things." Gregory settled into his seat with predatory grace and proceeded to ignore Barney. "We understand you've begun investigating the incident."

"That's correct. I put Didi's team in charge of this case."

Gregory's gaze flitted to the witch before finding mine. "And what conclusions have you reached so far?"

I shot a wary look at Didi and Samuel. They nodded slightly.

"It seems someone with extensive knowledge of the Amberford blood banks systematically robbed that facility," I said carefully. "They also stole the genealogical records of some very specific bloodlines."

Constantia's fingers tightened on her purse.

Gregory's expression didn't change.

"Do you have any suspects?" the vampire asked in a voice that gave little away.

"We're following a couple of leads," Didi admitted. She hesitated for a fraction of a second that didn't go unnoticed. "Your son Virgil was one of the last customers at Eternal Reserves before the break-in."

The silence became glacial.

I started to wish I'd never bothered to get out of bed this morning.

Bo gulped audibly, all thoughts of chasing his tail evidently abandoned.

# 8

# SUCKED DRY

GREGORY'S EYES FLASHED CRIMSON FOR A MOMENT. "I see."

"Virgil's alibi checks out," Gavin added hastily.

Constantia's jawline was so stiff I was surprised we couldn't hear her teeth grind.

"We also discovered a pattern of thefts at other blood banks throughout the town," I continued. "Most of which have gone unreported."

The air in the room grew so cold I was surprised my breath didn't mist in front of my face. Gregory's nails lengthened where he was gripping his arm rests, his eyes now a vivid scarlet.

Barney straightened in his chair.

The tension filtering through the mate bond had me glancing at Samuel.

His shoulders had bunched up, like he was ready to spring into action if Gregory tried anything stupid.

Constantia licked her lips nervously. "My dear, calm yourself."

Gregory ignored his wife. "Unreported?" His voice had taken on a dangerous edge.

"The facility managers were concerned about retribution," Didi said uncomfortably.

My pulse spiked when I felt power rise under Gregory's skin. It bloomed around him in a thick cloud that choked the air, the taste and smell starker than that of his son's.

Gavin and Didi flinched and shrank in their seats. Bo whimpered and dropped to the floor, his paws over his head.

I reached hastily for my inner wolf and urged her to do her nifty pacifier thing, my gaze focused unblinkingly on the vampire. My wolf let out a warning growl instead.

Gregory's eyes snapped to me. His canines lengthened, his expression growing ugly.

Great. I was about to be skewered by a vampire in front of my boyfriend, my dog, and my coworkers.

*"Enough!"*

The command cracked the air like thunder and made my wolf's ears flatten. My gaze snapped to Barney.

My mouth went dry.

The vampire's head practically brushed the ceiling where he suddenly loomed over Gregory. Shadows fluttered around him, forming a cape with a pointed collar that flickered in and out of view. His pupils were bloodred and radiated a chill that made Gavin's tail pop out and Bo whimper where he'd dived under my chair.

I swallowed. I hadn't even seen the vampire move.

A tiny gurgling sound issued from Gregory's throat. He made himself small in his chair.

Constantia was staring unblinkingly at Barney, her cheeks rosy and her eyes filled with undeniable hunger.

I had a sudden, stomach-churning suspicion about her history with Hawthorne & Associates's Head of Finance and Investments. From Didi's whole-body shudder, so did the witch.

"How about everyone relaxes before Gavin sets fire to the room?" Samuel ground out, amber lighting up his eyes where he'd risen to his feet.

Gavin's horns were fully out and his nostrils were sparking wildly.

Didi hastily moved some paperwork out of the dragon newt's range.

There was a knock at the door. Janet walked in without waiting for a reply, a tray of coffee and assorted pastries in hand.

"Refreshments, anyone?" the werewolf said with excessive brightness.

It was clear the HR Manager had been eavesdropping.

Samuel flashed a grateful look at her.

"Are there brain muffins?" Bo quavered.

Janet blinked, nonplussed. "No."

"Good. Because what just happened cured my constipation and brain muffins would definitely give me diarrhea."

The tension drained from the room like a deflated balloon.

My dog truly had a talent for cutting through supernatural drama.

Janet served the drinks and left. I could tell she was lurking outside.

Everyone now had a coffee except for a sulking Gavin, who was clutching a grape soda under Didi's supervision.

"You said you interviewed Virgil?" Constantia said, holding her cup like a life preserver.

"Yes." I could smell the concern in her scent despite her neutral tone.

"How is Virgil?" Gregory asked.

I narrowed my eyes a little at his supercilious expression.

Whereas Constantia seemed to want to know more about her estranged offspring, Gregory looked ready to condemn his son to burn at a fiery stake.

"He seems happy," I said coolly.

"Really?" Gregory's tone could have frozen Hell. "His career choice would suggest otherwise. Serving beverages to the masses sounds like my definition of purgatory."

My wolf's hackles rose. It was touch and go whether she was going to go for Gregory's throat.

I sensed Samuel's warning across our mate bond.

"Not everyone aspires to being a giant prick, Gregory," I said silkily.

Constantia's jaw sagged open. Samuel swallowed his coffee down the wrong pipe and began coughing violently. Didi and Gavin stared at me in wide-eyed admiration.

Or abject pity. It was hard to tell sometimes.

I knew I was taking my chances insulting a prominent member of the Amberford Alliance, but I'd had enough of the vampire's high-and-mighty attitude.

"You are correct, Abigail," Barney said coldly. He was back to his normal self, to the point where I almost believed I'd dreamed up his scary Lord of the Night performance. "There are indeed many pricks in the vampire world. Big pricks. Ugly pricks." He shot a steady look at Gregory. "Small pricks."

"Is that a ding-dong joke?" Bo intoned in a dramatic whisper that could probably be heard at the other end of the building. "Because I have a few of those."

"How about you keep those to yourself," Samuel said darkly, dabbing at his chin with a napkin. He looked around the room. "We should focus on the case."

"You mentioned you had a couple of leads," Gregory said frostily in the awkward silence. "What was the second one?"

"According to the ghouls at Eternal Reserves, the thief was humming Beethoven's Ninth Symphony," I replied more civilly.

Constantia paled. "Beethoven's Ninth Symphony?"

Gregory looked like he'd swallowed something sour.

Samuel furrowed his brow, his gaze swinging between the power couple. "Is there something you're not telling us?"

Constantia and Gregory traded a guarded look.

"Three prominent vampires were attacked last

night," Gregory admitted reluctantly. "That's part of the reason for our visit. They're all in Springhill General."

Samuel's shoulders knotted. Barney's eyes flashed crimson.

"Attacked?" Gavin swallowed convulsively. "Attacked how?" he quavered.

"Someone drained them almost to the bone," Gregory said flatly.

My stomach sank.

"They were barely alive when they were found," Constantia added in a small voice.

"What does that have to do with Beethoven's Ninth Symphony?" Didi asked, confused.

A sudden intuition blasted through me.

Gregory confirmed my hunch with his next words. "The victims all reported hearing classical music before the attack. It was Beethoven's Ninth Symphony."

A muscle twitched in Barney's jawline. The tension radiating off the Head of Finance and Investments was almost palpable. Somehow, I had a sneaky suspicion he knew more about this case than he was letting on.

Samuel steepled his hands under his chin and watched Gregory and Constantia closely.

"We need to interview the victims."

"Of course," Gregory said with a stiff nod. "I'll arrange it for tomorrow morning." He looked at his wife. "You might as well show it to them, dear."

"Show us what?" I asked warily.

Constantia opened her purse, withdrew a folded piece of paper, and passed it to Samuel, her knuckles white.

"We received this yesterday."

Samuel took the paper and unfolded it. His expression darkened.

"What is it?" I asked unenthusiastically.

"It's a blood purity manifesto."

Somehow, that didn't sound like a cocktail recipe.

Samuel handed me the paper stiffly. The others gathered around me.

Didi's eyes shrank to slits as she perused the letter. "Someone wants to cleanse the vampire community of inferior bloodlines?"

I studied the handwriting scrawled across the paper. It was elegant, old-fashioned, and completely unhinged.

"'The vampire race has been corrupted by centuries of mingling with lesser bloodlines,'" I read out loud. "'Only through purification can we return to our former glory. The weak must be culled so the strong may flourish. Look forward to a revival, my brethren!'"

It went on like this for three more paragraphs.

Bo emerged from under my chair, ears perking up and expression bright. "So I was right?!"

I grimaced at Gregory and Constantia's puzzled looks. "We were playing twenty guesses as to the culprit's motives. Bo came up with the 'wiping out inferior bloodlines' theory."

Gregory studied my dog with an inscrutable expression. I had the distinct feeling the Husky was either being measured for a coffin or a pedestal.

Bo withdrew quietly under my chair.

"I should warn you," Gregory said. "The vampires

who were attacked are not quite themselves at the moment. They may not be very cooperative."

Uncooperative vampires was right up there on the list of things I didn't want to have to deal with.

"What do you mean, exactly?" I asked carefully.

"Blood loss affects vampires differently than humans," Constantia explained. "They can become somewhat—theatrical. Sometimes, they even fall back on poetry and foreign languages."

Barney groaned. Gavin's nostrils issued a smoking signal of distress. Didi made a face.

I had a feeling this was going to be interesting for all the wrong reasons.

9

# A PINT TOO FAR

SPRINGHILL GENERAL STRADDLED A LOW HILL IN THE woods, north of the Crossroads. A foreboding dark limestone complex, it boasted buttresses, pointed arch windows, and gargoyles that seemed to leer down at anything approaching the heavy oak doors. Ivy crawled up the walls in brooding tangles and a central tower pierced the sky with dramatic flair.

All in all, the place looked like a Gothic monument to medical misery.

"This is so cool," Bo enthused, nails clicking on the stone steps we were climbing.

Gavin leaned closer to me. "Why does he look so happy?"

My mouth pressed to a thin line at the unhealthy gleam in the Husky's eyes.

"No doubt he's contemplating the various ways we could meet our demise inside this place so he can gossip about it on tonight's social howl."

Gavin looked hurt at this.

Bo wagged his tail innocently. "I think it would make for a great headline. It might even cheer Gus up."

"Who's Gus?" Didi asked with the gruesome fascination of someone watching a train wreck.

"The bulldog who lives across the road from Marshmallow."

"Who's Marsh—?" Didi started. "Never mind."

I hesitated, certain I wasn't going to like the answer but asking the question anyway. "What's wrong with Gus?"

"His humans got him fixed last week," Bo replied with the nonchalant air of a dog who was still in full possession of his meatballs. "He's been sulking about his lost masculine essence ever since. Rosie even brought him her favorite bone to make him feel better. You know, the one she dug up from the cemetery."

Barney curled a lip.

"Who's Rosie?" Gavin hissed.

"The Jack Russell who lives five doors down from Gus," I said absentmindedly.

"It's worrying how much you know about your dog's social life," Didi remarked.

Since we'd just entered the building, I decided to let that insult ride.

The interior of the hospital was fractionally more appealing than its outward appearance. Less *Frankenstein* and more *The Exorcist*. My wolf's nose twitched at the scents wafting through the building as we crossed a gloomy foyer and presented ourselves at reception.

The banshee behind the desk stiffened when we

explained the purpose of our visit. She spoke to a colleague in a low voice before coming around from behind the desk.

"This way, please. We've been expecting you."

Bo earned a side-eye as he strolled beside me.

"You know pets aren't allowed in the hospital, right?" the banshee said thinly.

"He's a service animal."

The banshee frowned at the Husky. "What kind of service does he offer?"

"Sass and muffin testing."

Bo straightened proudly.

The banshee escorted us to the ward where the vampire victims were being nursed back to health. To my surprise, the place was located in the basement and accessed through a service elevator that required a special key card.

"Is this standard protocol?" I asked uneasily as the doors closed on us.

"For these lunatics—I mean patients—yes," the banshee replied.

We emerged into what looked like a cross between a hospital and a medieval dungeon, complete with stone walls, wrought-iron light fixtures, and low-level moaning and groaning.

A trio of nurses huddled at a workstation up ahead. They were drawing straws with fraught expressions, like their lives depended on it. The shortest one, a dwarf, lost. She cursed and shook a tiny fist at the ceiling. Her werewolf and witch companions hastily pressed a tray into her hands, relieved.

"Looks like Hilda drew the short straw again," the banshee remarked as the dwarf turned and trudged down a hallway, beard drooping.

Gavin's nostrils smoked nervously. "What did Hilda lose at?"

"Giving Count de Vile his meds, probably."

"Oh God," Barney groaned.

The name sounded familiar.

"He's a longtime client of the firm," Didi said sourly at my questioning look. "Dave has to take antacids when he visits him."

Translated, the client was a pain in the ass.

The werewolf nurse noticed us first. She left the station and approached.

Recognition flared in her eyes at the sight of me. She swallowed and regained her composure.

"I'm afraid we're not accepting visitors right now."

"They're the people Mr. Tremaine called about," the banshee explained in a tone full of hidden meaning.

The werewolf's expression fell like a badly baked soufflé. "Oh." She chewed her lip. "You should come back tomorrow. Some of the victims are still, er, indisposed."

As if to prove her point, someone began wailing close by.

The werewolf's shoulders knotted.

A nurse with pointed ears and gossamer wings floated out of a room on the left, her expression harried and her uniform covered in stains that I hoped was pizza sauce.

"Could I have a hand?" the pixie started distractedly. "The baron is being—"

The wailing intensified, drowning out the rest of her words.

"Oh, woe is me!" someone lamented in the tone of one getting their innards ripped out. "To have witnessed what I have witnessed!"

"It's way too early for this shit," the banshee muttered under her breath.

Barney sighed heavily. "Not that pillock too."

"You know the baron?" I hazarded.

"For my sins."

The banshee departed hastily as the keening triggered more bemoaning and blubbering from several sources. The pixie fisted her hands and gnashed her teeth. The witch at the nurses' station popped a small bottle open and hastily downed a couple of pills, wincing.

"Look, now is really not a good time," the werewolf attempted again, desperation creeping into her voice. "How about I reschedule your visit for this afternoon at least—"

She was interrupted by a pale figure trailing dramatically out of a room on the right, one hand pressed to her forehead and the hem of her Victorian lace gown brushing the floor.

She was a middle-aged vampire with distinguished features and an obvious flair for histrionics. She brightened when she saw us.

"Ah, guests! Have you come to witness the tragic

tale of my demise? To hear how I was brought low by a fiend most foul?"

"This place is a loony bin," Bo huffed.

Most of Amberford's supernatural community was certifiable, but I decided to keep that opinion to myself.

The werewolf looked like she was reconsidering her career options as she hurried toward the vampire. "Lady Atkins, please return to your bed."

Lady Atkins was having none of this.

"My dear, I am but a shadow of my former self," she protested. "A mere specter haunting the ruins of what once was a magnificent vampire. Surely you will allow me the small comfort of sharing my sorrows with these strangers before I meet my maker?"

The pixie ground her teeth. "No one is meeting their maker."

Lady Atkins ignored her. Her eyes rounded when she noticed Barney. "Barnabas?"

"Muriel," the vampire greeted coolly.

"How lovely of you to grace us with your wonderful presence!" Lady Atkins batted her eyelids and blushed slightly.

Didi and I exchanged a look. Our vampire coworker was more of a Lothario than any of us had previously suspected.

"This is an official visit," Barney said coolly.

Lady Atkins deflated. "Oh."

"We need to ask you some questions about last night," Didi told the disappointed vampire.

A hair-raising ululation had us all freezing and

Gavin's horns popping out. Bo yelped and nearly stepped on the dragon newt's tail.

The sound had come from the depths of the ward.

# 10

# BAD BLOOD

THE WEREWOLF NURSE PALED. "OH, NO!" SHE TURNED and ran.

"You should give up, Joyce," the pixie muttered darkly, following. "Hilda's lost it."

"Don't do it, Hilda!" Joyce hollered. "He's not worth losing your license over! Irene, what are you waiting for?!"

The witch dashed out from behind the nurse's station and joined the pair as they pelted down the passage.

We exchanged an awkward glance as the sounds of their footsteps faded.

"Maybe we should go after them," I suggested.

"Do we have to?" Bo asked.

Gavin and Didi looked like they shared my dog's opinion.

Barney sighed. "Come on."

He led the way down the corridor, Lady Atkins following us at a cautious distance.

We traced the source of the altercation to a side room and found the nursing trio manhandling the dwarf nurse while the latter attempted valiantly to behead a vampire with a battleaxe twice her size.

"Let me at him!" she snarled, legs cycling a couple of feet off the floor.

The vampire on the bed scowled. "I must say, your behavior is most uncouth, sir."

"I'm a lady, you blood-sucking Neander—!" the dwarf growled before Irene muzzled her desperately with a hand.

"She's spunky," Bo commented, tail swinging.

Sometimes, I really missed my old job at Pennington & Graves.

Barney gave the vampire in the bed a dirty look. "What did you do, William?"

Count de Vile's gimlet gaze locked on Barney. His expression turned suspicious. "What are you doing here, Bludworth?"

"He's visiting," Lady Atkins simpered from the doorway.

"Trust me, I'd rather be anywhere else," Barney muttered.

Count de Vile curled a lip. "All I did was state the truth. The cuisine here leaves a lot to be desired. Why, my steak tartare was more tartare than steak and that Type-O wine might as well have been a Pinot Noir." He crossed his arms. "At this rate, I shall perish from starvation!"

The pixie's eyes flashed. "You've been here half a day. And this isn't a goddamn gourmet restaurant."

Count de Vile looked down his nose at her. "Watch your mouth, peasant." He sneered. "May I remind you that I pay that pittance you call a salary."

"Not from Dave's audits, you don't," Didi muttered.

The pixie closed her eyes. "Ugh, my blood pressure."

"Calm down, Hazel." Joyce turned to us, amber lighting up her eyes briefly in her distress. "As you can see, our patients are not in a position to—"

"I'm afraid this is rather urgent," Didi interrupted firmly.

I could tell the witch was trying hard not to turn everyone into a frog.

"Yeah, the sooner we do this, the sooner we can get out of this nuthouse," Gavin contributed.

"You said it, bro," Bo huffed.

"Do you have a room where we could interview the patients?" I asked Joyce diplomatically.

Count de Vile narrowed his eyes. "You smell like a Hawthorne, wolf. You must be that new luna of theirs." He scanned me from head to toe, like someone scrutinizing the best-by label on a block of moldy cheese. "You look like you're of common stock. Victoria must be disappointed."

Bo stamped his feet. "How rude!"

My wolf's hackles rose a little. "Victoria and I get along fine, not that it's any of your business."

"Yeah, and Pearl is my bestie," Bo huffed indignantly.

"Bestie" was stretching it, but I decided not to point this out to my dog.

Count de Vile arched a haughty eyebrow.

"Somehow I doubt that. Those two have high standards."

A low growl left my throat.

Joyce evidently sensed I was about to go she-wolf on her patient and hastily arranged to bring the three victims to a treatment room.

Baron Philippe Beaumont was wheeled in on a gurney, still wailing. He stopped abruptly at the sight of us.

"Barnabas?" he quavered.

"Philippe," Barney grunted.

"Oh Barnabas!" Baron Beaumont sat up weakly. "It is good to see you, *mon ami*. Come, let me tell you about my woes."

"I'd rather you didn't."

"But Hell is empty and all the devils are here," the baron protested.

Bo's tail started wagging. "I like him. He's like that guy from my favorite TV show."

"*Murder, She Barked?*" I asked automatically.

"*Buried Secrets and Biscuit Treats.*"

Didi's left eye started twitching.

Lady Atkins gave my dog a wary look before addressing Beaumont a tad sharply. "He's here to listen to all our woes, Philippe, not just yours."

"Yes, so how about you put a sock in it," Count de Vile grumbled.

Baron Beaumont bristled. "Do not speak to me, sir," he snapped. "Why, more of your conversation would surely infect my brain!"

I was impressed by the flying thespian insults despite myself.

I heard teeth grinding and shot a glance at Didi.

The witch looked like she was five minutes away from saying to hell with it all and transforming everyone into an amphibian.

"The Tremaines asked Hawthorne & Associates to investigate a series of blood bank robberies," I told the assembled vampires hastily. "We suspect the one who attacked the three of you last night was behind them."

Lady Atkins clutched her nonexistent pearls. "A robbery, you say?!"

"Robberies," Gavin corrected.

"Madre de dios," Baron Beaumont murmured, ashen-faced.

Count de Vile lowered his brows. "Does this mean the blood banks in Amberford are running low?"

I could see why Dave popped antacids when he had to pay this guy a visit.

"Oh, no." Lady Atkins had gone as pale as a ghost. "Please don't tell me this is going to be like that time in the 1980, when we had to survive on kale for six months?!"

"There was a blood-borne virus going around," Gavin explained at my puzzled expression. "We learned about it in school."

Bo shuddered. "I hate kale."

"Tell me about it," Lady Atkins mumbled.

Barney steered the conversation back on track. "Gregory told us you were in your own homes when it happened. Can you tell us more?"

The three victims exchanged an uncomfortable glance.

"There's not much to say." Count de Vile scowled. "That scoundrel broke into our bedrooms and sucked us dry while we slept."

We stared.

"That's it?" I asked skeptically.

Didi frowned. "You're all powerful vampires. How could one man immobilize you and drain you of over half your blood volume without you putting up so much as a fight?"

"Well, if you must know, mademoiselle," Baron Beaumont started in a friendly voice, "the perpetrator moved like a wraith—"

"A shadow," Lady Atkins interrupted, bobbing her head firmly.

"Indeed," Baron Beaumont continued with a trace of irritation. "A creature of the night more terrible than myself."

Count de Vile sneered. "There are stray dogs more terrible than you."

"Is there anything useful you wish to contribute to this conversation, William?" Barney said icily while Baron Beaumont spluttered. "Or are you just flapping those bloodless lips of yours?"

Count de Vile waved a hand vaguely. "He was fast. And the reason we couldn't fight back is because of what he did to immobilize us."

My scalp prickled. "Immobilize you?"

I glanced at the others, a vision of the crystal skull rising at the back of my mind. From Didi's and

Gavin's looks, they were having similar morbid thoughts.

"In darkness deep, a predator came," Lady Atkins recited solemnly, "with Beethoven's tune and bloodred flame. He pierced my flesh with needle bright and stole away my precious might—"

"So he really was humming Beethoven's Ninth Symphony?" Barney cut in sharply.

I furrowed my brow. "Wait. He used a needle?!"

Lady Atkins deflated. "Yes and yes," she confirmed a smidgen sullenly.

"He injected something into our necks," Count de Vile grunted. "It must have been some kind of drug. It drained us of our strength and pretty much paralyzed us."

My mouth went dry.

A muscle jumped in Barney's jawline. "There are not many drugs that can paralyze a vampire." Unease underscored his words.

"Some clever Dick obviously came up with one," Count de Vile said darkly. "Amberford is full of them, after all."

Gavin's horns had popped out and his nostrils were sparking alarmingly. "So not only do we have a psychotic ancient vampire intent on purifying his race going around Amberford doing God knows what, we're also dealing with a narcotics case?"

Baron Beaumont blinked slowly. "Purifying his race?"

Didi shot a dirty look at Gavin. I swallowed a sigh.

Bo plopped down on his haunches. "The cat's out of the bag now."

Count de Vile's eyes had shrunk to slits. "Don't tell me that quack wrote some kind of blood purity manifesto?"

"He did." Barney shrugged at Didi's glare. "They were going to find out soon anyway. Gregory has a duty to inform them."

"Can you describe the man who attacked you?" I asked warily.

"Tall, as pale as moonlight, dressed as though he'd stepped out of a daguerreotype," Count de Vile said promptly.

"His eyes were as red as fresh blood," Baron Beaumont contributed with a shiver.

I sighed. That could be any vampire.

"Anything else?"

Lady Atkins fidgeted with the neckline of her gown.

"What is it, Muriel?" Barney asked.

"My memory is hazy, but I think I heard him say some strange things before he left."

My pulse quickened. "What kind of strange things?"

"He told me my bloodline showed promise," the vampire replied uneasily. "That I was contributing to something greater."

Baron Beaumont cleared his throat. "I recall similar words. He said he was creating something special." He hesitated. "That Amberford would soon witness the birth of a new age of vampire supremacy."

The hairs rose on the back of my neck. Barney went very still.

The vampires had little else to add, so we left them in the care of Joyce and her coworkers and drove back to Hawthorne & Associates in grim silence. My phone pinged with an incoming message when we were halfway across town. I frowned when I read it.

"Samuel wants to see us when we get back."

"Now what?" Didi muttered.

# 11

# A GRAVE SITUATION

SAMUEL WAS WAITING FOR US IN THE FOYER OF THE building.

One look at his expression told me we were in for more unwelcome news.

"Lord Chudwell was found dead at his estate this morning," he said without preamble. "Gregory called. The coroner just informed him."

Didi gasped. Gavin squeaked. Bo's ears flattened.

Barney froze. "Giles is dead? That's impossible!"

"Who's Lord Chudwell?" I asked nervously.

"He's from one of the purest bloodlines in New England," the vampire replied. His voice carried a note I hadn't heard before. "His family tree goes back to the original vampire settlers."

My wolf stirred uneasily. Our case had just taken a dark undertone none of us had been expecting.

"Was it another attack?" I asked in the fraught hush.

"It appears so." Samuel's jaw tightened, his emotions making my wolf fidget as they filtered through the mate bond. "Though this one went considerably worse for the victim."

"He was probably targeted because of his bloodline, right?" Didi said quietly.

Though he wasn't showing it, it was clear the news had upset Barney.

Samuel rubbed the back of his neck. "The coroner suspects his death was an accident. She's still at the scene. I want you to get over there before the Vampire Council descends and turns this whole thing into a political circus."

I stared. "There's a Vampire Council?"

This was news to me. Then again, I'd only been a werewolf for one hot second.

"There are many councils in Amberford," my alpha admitted reluctantly.

"Think of them as the equivalent of a homeowners association," Didi said with distaste. "Lots of rules, endless meetings, and an unhealthy obsession with property values."

Winter clouds had darkened the heavens by the time we got to Temple Heights. The Chudwell estate loomed under the overcast sky at the end of a long tree-lined driveway.

The place had the signature Amberford look, ergo it looked like it had been designed by someone from the Middle Ages who had severe commitment issues. The main house was an architectural fever dream of towers and turrets that reminded me faintly of Château Montmartre. Except for the gargoyles. Those guys were perched on every available surface and wore expressions of perpetual indigestion.

"Someone had money to burn," I observed tactfully as we pulled up a circular drive.

"And highly questionable taste." Didi stared at a particularly hideous gargoyle that appeared to be picking its nose.

Bo pressed his face to the car window and wagged his tail. "Do you think any of them come alive at night?"

Samuel rolled his eyes at the Husky's gruesomely hopeful tone as he parked the Bentley. We exited the car.

The fact that the Hawthorne alpha had decided to accompany us had come as a surprise. It felt weird having my boyfriend along on a case.

It was also making my insides flutter in all kinds of ways. I found myself studying his perfectly formed behind with focused concentration as we approached the mansion.

"Abby?" my alpha said awkwardly.

"Yes, Samuel?"

"How about you dial down those thoughts?"

I flushed a little under the others' leaden stares. "Sorry."

Bo studied me warily. "Pearl was right about you."

"Why, what did Pearl say?"

"That you have a one-track mind. And that Samuel's headstone will probably say 'Died while bravely performing his conjugal duties.'"

Samuel missed a step and almost stumbled. Didi curled a lip.

Seeing as I couldn't exactly deny Pearl's claim, I decided not to rise to the secondhand insult.

A trio of figures was waiting for us on the porch. Two of them looked familiar.

Officer Brigham paled a little at the sight of me.

"Hello," the werewolf said nervously.

The last time I'd seen him, he'd been squatting on his superior officer, both the unfortunate victims of my actions at the Holts' ball.

Detective Johnson—said superior officer in question—stood beside Officer Brigham. He scrutinized my hands.

"I am relieved to see you are missing your crystal skull tonight, Miss West," the werewolf grunted.

I was never going to hear the end of that story.

A woman in a practical gray suit stared at me curiously. She had short purple hair and the kind of no-nonsense expression that suggested she'd seen it all and wasn't impressed by any of it.

"Samuel," she greeted with a curt nod.

"Rita." Samuel made the introductions. "Abby, this is Rita Frank, the supernatural coroner for this district."

We shook hands.

"It's a pleasure to meet the new Hawthorne luna." There was a slight echo to the coroner's voice.

"Are you a—?" I paused awkwardly.

"A banshee?" Rita said with a dry smile. "Yes, retired. Turns out a career in wailing prepared me well for dealing with the recently deceased and their grieving relatives."

"I like her attitude," Bo huffed.

Officer Brigham and Detective Johnson observed the Husky warily.

Rita gave my dog a steady look. "I see he's as entertaining as the rumors say he is."

Bo's ears perked up.

"There are rumors about me?" he enthused, tail swinging like crazy.

Rita politely declined to answer and led us into the mansion's grand foyer, Officer Brigham staying put at the entrance to keep watch. The entrance hall was crowded with oil paintings of stern-faced vampires who looked like they'd spent their immortal lives complaining about taxes.

"The victim was found at the bottom of the main staircase." The banshee indicated the impressive marble structure sweeping upward in dramatic curves from the middle of the entrance hall. "He died of a broken neck, followed by an accidental decapitation. A surprising way for a vampire to go, if I say so myself." She shot a contrite glance at Barney.

"Accidental decapitation?" I asked nervously.

Rita pointed at a suit of armor with a bloodied sword standing guard next to the staircase. "He bounced and sliced his head right off that."

"How, er, unfortunate," I murmured glassily.

"But way cool," Bo enthused with macabre enthusiasm.

Barney frowned. "I still can't believe Giles is dead. Are you certain?"

"He's been as cold as ice for going on eight hours, so yes." Rita sighed at Barney's look. "Look, I understand your skepticism. A decapitation should have been a walk in the park for a vampire to recover from, but there is no denying that he's as dead as a doorknob."

Barney's face grew shuttered.

Samuel frowned at the staircase. "He fell the whole way?"

"All forty-three steps," Detective Johnson confirmed.

Rita led us to where yellow tape cordoned off the base of the stairs. A chalk outline marked where Lord Chudwell's body had been found.

The angle of the limbs made my stomach twist and Gavin heave a little. A grim circle a few feet away marked where the head had landed.

"Gregory told me what happened to the vampires in Springhill General," Rita said, matter-of-fact. "The attacker used the same MO. I found injection marks on Lord Chudwell's neck and evidence of significant blood loss. Unlike the others though, he appears to have fought back."

Barney stirred. "How can you tell?"

"Torn fabric caught on the banister, defensive wounds on his hands, and"—Rita paused and pursed her lips like she was about to reveal a dirty secret—"he was found clutching this." She reached inside a metal case filled with forensic tools and produced an evidence bag containing what appeared to be a very old and very worn teddy bear with its belly ripped open and stuffing spilling out. "It seems he used this to try and protect himself."

It was the saddest thing I had ever seen.

"That's Mr. Snuggles," Barney said stiffly. "Giles has had him since he was human."

"Shall we continue?" Detective Johnson grunted.

Rita nodded briskly. "The attack appears to have taken place in the victim's private study. Let me show you."

She led us up a side staircase to avoid the crime scene. The study was on the second floor, with views over the extensive gardens at the rear of the property. There were heavy curtains at the windows, multiple locks on the cabinets lining the walls, and enough security cameras to make a casino jealous. The place was also a mess.

I took in the paperwork and overturned objects strewn across the floor.

"What did Lord Chudwell do for a living?"

"Nothing that would warrant this level of security," Rita said.

"He lived off the interest of his investment portfolio and the properties and land he owned here and abroad," Barney murmured glumly.

Detective Johnson furrowed his brow. "The strange thing is, none of the security equipment was disabled. It all just stopped working when the attacker arrived."

That sounded uncomfortably familiar.

"All of it?" Didi asked insistently.

"Every single device," Rita confirmed. "Almost like something interfered with the electronics."

Samuel's expression darkened. "Were there any witnesses?"

"Two," Detective Johnson replied. "The housekeeper and the butler. They're waiting in the servants' quarters."

Rita guided us there and introduced the housekeeper first.

Mrs. Betsy Clark was exactly what you might expect from a ghoul who'd spent decades working for vampire aristocracy. Her gray skin was impeccably maintained, her uniform spotless, and her demeanor suggested she could organize a dinner party for fifty while simultaneously disposing of inconvenient bodies.

"Lord Chudwell was such a refined gentleman." She dabbed at her eyes with a handkerchief and blew her nose noisily. "Always said please and thank you when he asked me to make him a Bloody Mary. Very considerate."

"Does she mean a Bloody Mary or a *bloody* Mary?" Bo whispered.

Didi and I hushed him. Detective Johnson looked like he was having second thoughts about taking on this case.

"About this morning," Samuel prompted gently while Betsy sniffed. "Can you tell us what happened?"

"I was in the kitchen preparing Lord Chudwell's breakfast when I heard music and my master shouting from the front of the house."

"Beethoven's Ninth Symphony," Didi said grimly.

Betsy nodded tearfully.

"Did you see the attacker?" I asked.

"I only caught a glimpse of him when I ran into the entrance hall. He was a tall gentleman in a vintage coat. Moved like a dancer." She furrowed her brow a little, her tone turning stringent. "Much better posture than these modern vampires with their scruffy outfits and their slouching."

An image of Virgil rose immediately to my mind.

Barney's expression had grown increasingly troubled while the ghoul spoke.

Quincy the butler was a different story entirely. Whereas Mrs. Clark was moderately chatty, the vampire still seemed shell-shocked by his master's passing and kept wringing his hands.

"The master had received letters," he quavered, his pale eyes swinging nervously between us. "Threats. I pressed him to inform the authorities, but he refused and burned them all."

My shoulders knotted. None of the other victims had reported receiving sinister correspondence.

"What did the letters say?" Barney asked tensely.

Quincy gulped at the vampire's grim expression.

"They were from someone claiming to be an old friend." The butler faltered. "He said he wanted to meet Master Chudwell to talk about the old ways. That— that Master *had* to help him change things for the vampire community."

I recalled the words from the blood purity manifesto the Tremaines had received with a degree of dread.

"Did the letters have a return address?" Samuel asked.

"No, sir."

Didi was furiously scribbling notes. "And Lord Chudwell never mentioned this man's name?"

"No, miss."

I frowned. This sounded more and more like our suspect had been playing a long game.

"Is there anything else we should know?" I asked.

Quincy's pale gaze met mine. "I told Detective Johnson that the cats saw everything. You should talk to them."

I stared, nonplussed. "What cats?"

Detective Johnson made a face. "Yeah, about that."

# 12

# HERDING CATS

"I can't believe I'm being made to work," Pearl sneered where she sat regally on Victoria's lap.

"It's about time you started earning your keep," Samuel said coldly as he pulled up to Lord Chudwell's estate for the second time in as many days. "That gourmet food you inhale regularly doesn't pay for itself."

"There's no need to be unpleasant, Samuel," Victoria protested. "You know Pearl is the glue holding our family together."

Pearl looked briefly ambivalent about being compared to something that used to be made from horses' hooves.

"Yeah," Bo said beside me, his tail thumping against the car door in solidarity with the cat. "It's not Pearl's fault she acts like a stuck-up queen. She was born that way."

Pearl narrowed her eyes dangerously at my dog.

"How about everyone calm down?" I sighed.

It wasn't even nine o'clock yet and I could already feel a headache brewing.

The previous evening had ended in a complete disaster.

Lord Chudwell's three Persian cats had taken one look at our investigative team and decided we were beneath their notice. They'd spent the entire twenty minutes of our attempt at an interview perched on their velvet chaise longue, occasionally deigning to sniff dismissively in our direction in a way that made it clear that speaking to mere mortals was a grave insult to their aristocratic sensibilities. Doubly so if said mortals were of common stock.

Rita had tried hard to hold her laughter back at this unexpected development, but being a banshee made this difficult and the halls of the mansion had echoed with shrill cackling for some time, much to Betsy's and Quincy's dismay. Even Detective Johnson had been unable to hide a satisfied smile at the fact we got the same treatment as him.

"They actually turned their backs on us," Gavin had complained afterward. "All three of them. In *unison*." The dragon newt's nostrils had smoked indignantly.

"Like a synchronized swimming team," Bo had added glumly. "But with more attitude. And claws." My dog's attempts at interspecies diplomacy had fallen flat and almost earned him a deadly nose boop.

"I've interviewed hostile witnesses before, but never ones who literally presented me with their rear ends," Didi had muttered darkly.

The cats had remained stubbornly silent

throughout our visit, communicating only through tail swishes and the odd disdainful meow. Which was why we were now back at the estate, armed with Pearl and what we hoped was a foolproof plan.

Didi, Barney, and Gavin were waiting for us in the foyer, along with Detective Johnson. They stiffened a little at the sight of Victoria and Pearl. Polite greetings were exchanged, after which my coworkers and the detective breathed a sigh of relief.

Betsy appeared. The housekeeper's gray skin had taken on a slightly green tinge, which I was learning was the ghoul equivalent of breaking out in hives.

"Their Ladyships are being particularly difficult this morning," she said anxiously. "Ever since they heard you were bringing—reinforcements." She shot a nervous glance at Pearl.

Pearl was surveying the mansion with the air of someone conducting a property inspection.

"I'm sure Pearl will manage them just fine," Victoria reassured.

"You and me both, lady," Detective Johnson said under his breath. "I don't want to write another report about uncooperative feline witnesses."

"I'm telling you, Fur Ball," Bo whined at Pearl, "these cats are very snooty."

"No one in New England is snootier than I," Pearl declared haughtily.

"She has a point," I said solemnly.

Pearl's eyes shrank to slits.

Quincy the vampire butler emerged from a hallway before things could deteriorate into an all-out cat fight.

"Their Ladyships are ready to receive you in the blue drawing room," he announced in a hushed voice. He hesitated. "I've prepared some fresh salmon, just in case."

"So we can smother them with it?" Didi asked nastily.

Detective Johnson started looking antsy. Barney began tapping a foot. Gavin was trying to push his horns back in.

"Let's get this show on the road," Samuel said in a hard voice.

I wanted to warn my alpha this could turn into a satire but decided to hold my tongue. Nobody needed extra sass this morning.

We followed the housekeeper and the butler to the blue drawing room.

Samuel stayed slightly behind me, either out of a protective urge or because it was a strategic position for making a quick exit if the cat interview went sideways. Given our track record with Lord Chudwell's pets so far, I couldn't exactly blame him. Besides, he had enough feline-related drama to contend with at home without having to suffer it at work too.

Betsy took a deep breath and opened the doors with the look of someone defusing a bomb.

We peered inside a room decorated in all shades of blue. The three Persian cats were arranged on yet another chaise longue, this one covered in indigo damask.

Bella, the white one with the pink bow, sat in the

center. She was flanked by the silver tabby Coco and the cream-colored Truffles. All three had their tails wrapped primly around their paws and wore expressions that suggested they were personally offended by our very existence.

"Anyone else think they look like a firing squad?" Detective Johnson asked nervously.

Samuel and I hushed him.

Undaunted by the three cats' withering stares, Victoria stepped forward.

"Allow me to present Lady Veronica Pearl Whiskerton the Third."

"Whiskerton?" Detective Johnson hissed. "Really?!"

Didi stepped on his foot.

Pearl ignored the detective and leapt down gracefully from Victoria's arms. The Persian cats' eyes narrowed in unison as she approached the chaise longue.

"I understand you witnessed yesterday's unpleasantness," Pearl started without preamble, her voice carrying a note of authority I'd only ever heard once before, at the Holts' ball. "Now, how about you stop being difficult and tell these people what they want to know."

An icy silence descended upon the drawing room. Gavin gulped audibly. Didi's knuckles whitened around her pen and notepad. Victoria looked pleased.

Bella lifted her chin.

"And you are?" she asked in a voice dripping with contempt.

"Someone who outranks you." Pearl sat down and began grooming her paw with deliberate nonchalance.

The temperature in the room dropped several degrees.

I was impressed despite myself.

Unfortunately, Lord Chudwell's cats weren't.

"I beg your pardon?" Coco's voice had icebergs that could have sunk an ocean liner.

"You heard me," Pearl drawled. "I'm a Hawthorne pack familiar. You're pets. The hierarchy is crystal clear."

Truffles hissed and arched her back. "How dare you—?!"

"Shut it." Pearl fixed the cat with a stare that could have frozen boiling water. "Let me make something clear. The reason I'm being made to suffer this indignity instead of having a well-deserved nap on a radiator right now is because you three were too busy being precious to help solve a murder yesterday. Your owner is dead and you appear more concerned with your wounded pride than finding his killer."

The three Persian cats went from haughty to visibly uncomfortable.

"She's good at this," I muttered.

"Decades of practice," Victoria said.

"Can I borrow her sometime?" Detective Johnson asked in a low voice. "Some of our perps can be tight-lipped."

Bo placed a sympathetic paw on the police officer's leg. "You can't afford Pearl."

A tense standoff was happening across the way.

The silence stretched until even I felt compelled to confess to something.

Bella finally cracked.

"The intruder had a briefcase," the cat said reluctantly.

We leaned forward attentively, Didi with her notepad.

"It was black leather," Truffles added reluctantly. "Nice quality. Italian, I think."

"Did you see what was inside it?" I asked.

Bella shot a wary glance at Pearl and shifted uncomfortably. "Vials. Small glass vials filled with blood."

Didi's pen stopped moving. Samuel's expression sharpened. Victoria started looking a little green around the gills.

"How many vials?" Barney asked quietly.

"Dozens," Coco admitted. "They were labeled, but he moved too quickly for us to make out anything useful."

Truffles's ears twitched. "I did spot a name on one of the tubes though," the cat confessed reluctantly. Her eyes flicked warily to Barney. "It said Maximus Dorian Bludworth."

"Oh my," Victoria mumbled.

A frozen hush fell around the room.

We all looked worriedly at Barney, Detective Johnson the most nervous of our group. The vampire's eyes were glowing crimson and his nails were scoring thin lines in his palms.

"That's my great-uncle," he ground out, his voice

carrying a troubling echo of the power he'd wielded when he'd subdued Gregory.

I hesitated, the smell of the vampire's blood making my wolf fidget.

"Is he—?" I trailed off awkwardly.

Barney took a shuddering breath and forced himself to relax. "Alive, last I heard."

"Was there anything else?" Samuel asked the cats stiffly in the fraught silence.

"There was a pamphlet," Bella said. "In the case."

I stared. "What kind of pamphlet?"

"It was for a funeral parlor." Bella's tail swished hesitantly. "Pinevale."

Betsy made a strangled sound, her gray skin now completely green. She swayed slightly. Quincy moved to steady her.

"That's where Master Chudwell's funeral is going to be held tomorrow afternoon," the butler mumbled.

Bo's eyes brightened. "I smell a clue!" He sniffed the air. "And salmon. I definitely smell salmon."

The butler awkwardly extracted a sandwich bag stuffed with fresh salmon fillets from his pocket. Lord Chudwell's cats' eyes brightened with thinly masked interest.

I lowered my brows. Bo was right. This couldn't be a coincidence.

"Why would a vampire be carrying a pamphlet for a funeral home?" Gavin asked, puzzled.

"Maybe he was going to check it out for himself?" Detective Johnson asked with a grimace. "You know, make future arrangements?"

"Vampires are known for being organized like that," Victoria confirmed.

"You're certain it was Pinevale?" Samuel asked the cats.

"We can read," Bella said with wounded dignity. "And there were pictures. You know, coffins, flowers. Morbid-looking graves."

Pearl was watching the cats with narrowed eyes. "There's something you're not telling us."

I blinked, surprised.

For a moment, the three Persians looked like they were going to deny the claim. They gave in to Pearl's stringent stare and huddled together for a whispered conference.

Bella finally spoke. "The man who attacked our master. He smelled wrong."

Samuel stilled. "Wrong how?"

"Like—like old things. You know, museums and dusty books. And power."

Truffles wrinkled her nose. "Dark power."

We traded wary looks. That wasn't ominous at all.

"I think we should attend Lord Chudwell's funeral," I suggested.

Didi nodded. Barney clenched his jaw.

Detective Johnson raised an eyebrow. "Stakeout?"

"Oh, I like those," Gavin enthused, nostrils smoking.

"I don't," Bo complained.

Samuel frowned and rubbed his chin. "It would be better if some of us attended as guests."

"That sounds eminently sensible," Victoria agreed.

"I can add you to the guest list," Quincy said where he was still propping up a green Betsy.

"We would appreciate it," Samuel said gratefully.

"Anyone else think this funeral is doomed?" Bella whispered as we turned to leave.

"Probably," Coco agreed.

"Definitely," Truffles corrected.

At that point in my life, I had no idea exactly how true their predictions would turn out to be.

13

# DEATH BECOMES HIM

Pinevale Funeral Parlor loomed against the gray sky amidst the otherwise pleasant, middle-class landscape of west Amberford. It was the epitome of a business that catered exclusively to the undead: old, imposing, and about as cheerful as spending a night in a graveyard.

"This place seems fun," I observed reluctantly as we pulled into the parking lot on Thursday afternoon.

Bo's tail drooped. "I've seen morgues with more personality."

"He watched CSI: Doghouse last night," I said at Samuel's faint frown.

"Too much TV will rot your brain," Samuel told my dog.

"I fear it's already too late for that canine," Pearl said with a sniff. "Some brain muffins might help him recover."

Bo curled a lip like he'd just caught a whiff of a skunk who'd spent a week hugging garbage in a sauna.

Victoria pretended not to hear our conversation and adjusted her black hat with the efficiency of someone who'd attended far too many supernatural funerals.

"Remember, we're here to pay our respects. Please refrain from doing anything that will disgrace the family name."

I couldn't help but sense that remark had been intended for me.

"You do realize this is an undercover operation involving the police, right?"

Victoria narrowed her eyes. "An operation that you will carry out with honor and integrity."

I was about to point out that honor and integrity were not exactly my forte when our earpieces crackled.

"For the love of— Gavin, stop breathing on the camera lens!" Didi snapped over the comm.

"Sorry, I get nervous at funerals," the dragon newt said guiltily.

"You've been to exactly one funeral," the witch pointed out.

"Yeah and someone tried to sacrifice me to a goat demon," Gavin protested. "Forgive me if I'm a little anxious."

"I should have stayed in regular police work," Detective Johnson muttered.

Victoria's eyes glazed over while Samuel did his best to pretend this was normal undercover talk.

"Look on the bright side," I said with an encouraging smile. "It can't get any worse than the Holts' ball."

Pearl swished her tail. "Those are brave words coming from someone who's less than a week away from her next white wolf transformation."

I patted my hair self-consciously. I could already feel the pull of the next full moon and had to resort to using my Moon Shine: Extra Glossy Coat shampoo this morning to tame my wild locks.

"You look fine," Samuel reassured as we climbed out of the Bentley.

I smoothed down my new black dress. "Are you sure?"

"Yes." His eyes grew heated. "You should wear that on our next date."

Warmth flooded my cheeks. I bit my lip.

Our last date had ended with us driving to a remote rest stop and testing the Bentley's suspension late into the night.

Victoria sighed. "Look, while I appreciate that you're on the cusp of your relationship, you should show your respect for the dead."

"Sorry," Samuel and I mumbled.

"Are they always like this?" Detective Johnson asked over the comm.

"We have a betting pool going on how long it will take for Abby to break Samuel's desk," Didi replied in a tone holding mild disgust.

My mouth pressed to a thin line as we navigated the crowded parking lot. I definitely needed to have a word with Fred.

It had dawned on me recently that Samuel and I spent a worrying amount of time naked when we were in each other's company. To my relief, Caroline had revealed that the first year of a newly mated werewolf couple's life pretty much centered around getting to know one another in the biblical sense. She'd gone on to describe how she and her husband Kent had broken more inn beds around New England than any werewolf couple she knew, a morsel of information I could have done without but which I nonetheless accepted graciously.

The unmarked van where Didi, Gavin, and Detective Johnson were monitoring the funeral was parked across the street and looked poorly disguised where it lurked behind a newspaper delivery truck. Even from here, I could make out Gavin's horns through the windshield.

"They're about as subtle as a brick through a window," Pearl observed tartly. "At this rate, I doubt they'll spot the suspect even if he does show up."

"Should I go over there and give them tips?" Bo suggested helpfully.

Samuel swallowed a sigh.

Victoria gave me final instructions as we approached the entrance.

"Supernatural funerals have very specific protocols," she explained sternly. "Do not comment on the deceased's appearance and under no circumstances should you touch anything."

"What about shaking hands with the other guests?" I hazarded.

"Most of the attendees will be vampires. They don't shake hands. They air-kiss."

"Right," I muttered.

We made our way inside the funeral parlor and joined a small crowd of mourners in the foyer. I looked around curiously, my wolf rousing at the complex scents and emotions swarming the air around us.

The vampire aristocracy was out in force. They were all dressed in expensive black attire and stood in tiny clusters speaking in hushed tones, a few occasionally dabbing at dry eyes with silk handkerchiefs.

To my surprise, I'd learned that vampires couldn't cry. Hugh had claimed this was because of a physical impediment. Pearl had declared it was because they were cold-hearted bastards that would as soon kill you as look at you.

"Poor Giles," a vampire with a monocle said in a low voice. "He was such a refined gentleman."

A woman in an elaborate black dress with a veil that could have doubled as a fishing net blew her nose discreetly next to him. "He was taken far too soon."

"Hear, hear," another man muttered.

Barney appeared from the direction of the parlor's main room.

"I've secured our seats."

A ripple of unease ran through the gathered mourners at his sight.

It was clear the assembled vampires were as wary of Barney as Gregory had been.

We followed him into the funeral parlor's main room.

Lord Chudwell's coffin sat on a shallow stage at the

front, surrounded by enough flowers to stock a small garden center. The casket was covered in gold trim and what looked like genuine gemstones.

"Are those real?" Detective Johnson asked dubiously over the comm.

They were monitoring the inside of the funeral home through the tiny camera brooches pinned to our clothes.

"By the looks of it, yes," I muttered.

"Vampires don't do subtle," Victoria said.

That was becoming unmistakably clear.

I spotted the Tremaines talking to a woman near the front row.

"That's Aubrey Sweeney, the owner and director of Pinevale," Victoria murmured. "She's a banshee."

Betsy, Quincy, and the cats were in the family section to the left of the stage. The housekeeper and the butler acknowledged us with stiff nods. The cats ignored us.

Gregory and Constantia greeted us politely when we took our seats beside them. Bo's bow tie earned a brief stare.

The room was filling up with more mourners. I spotted several familiar faces from vampire high society, all of whom were making a great show of their grief while simultaneously checking out each other's outfits.

The funeral director waited until everyone was seated before approaching the podium to begin the service.

"Dear friends, we are gathered here today to honor

the memory of Lord Giles Pilkington Chudwell," she began in a voice that carried just a hint of her supernatural nature. "A vampire of distinguished lineage and impeccable taste."

"The gargoyles on his estate would disagree," Pearl muttered.

Bo grinned, tail swishing. "They were cool, though. In a poop-inducing kinda way."

Gregory narrowed his eyes. Samuel's mouth flattened to a thin line.

"Lord Chudwell lived a long and fulfilling undead life," the banshee continued shrilly, doing her best to ignore the cat and the dog. "I shall now invite his acquaintances to say a few words about him."

The service progressed with various vampires taking to the podium to share memories of the deceased. To Bo's delight, most of these seemed to involve dinner parties, investment portfolios, and the occasional blood duel.

"He once challenged the Duke of Carlyle to a sword fight over a disputed wine vintage," one elderly vampire recalled fondly. "Giles won, naturally."

"What vintage?" another vampire called out.

"1847 Bordeaux."

A murmur of approval rippled through the crowd.

I was beginning to understand why vampires had such complicated social lives.

To my surprise, Barney didn't take to the podium. I couldn't help but feel he was still in denial about his friend's death.

The banshee finally called for anyone who wished

to pay their final respects to approach the casket. I rose along with Victoria, Samuel, and the Tremaines and joined the mourners shuffling into a queue in the center aisle.

Betsy and Quincy stood at the front, handing out red roses.

Bo padded alongside me as I approached the ornate coffin, flower in hand. It was my first time seeing Lord Chudwell.

He was a distinguished-looking vampire even in death and had a kind face and laughter lines around his eyes that spoke of an undead life well lived. Someone had stitched up Mr. Snuggles and laid the teddy bear beside him. The stitches matched the neat row on Lord Chudwell's neck.

I had just placed the flower inside the casket when the hairs rose on the back of my neck. My wolf had just gone on alert.

I was pretty certain I'd seen the body twitch.

Samuel stopped where he was making his way back to his seat, no doubt sensing the sudden tension humming through me across the mate bond.

I frowned and leaned in closer to take a look at the dead vampire.

"Abby, what are you—?" Didi started suspiciously in my ear.

Lord Chudwell sneezed.

14

# DEAD WRONG

A STRANGLED "GAH!" LEFT ME.

Didi gasped in my ear.

Victoria and Constantia gurgled. The funeral director sucked in air, her hair uncoiling around her head like a spring. Samuel and Gregory swore. Barney's eyes rounded. Pearl stared unblinkingly.

A stunned hush fell over the funeral parlor.

Didi, Gavin, and Detective Johnson started shouting in my ears.

I startled and reflexively gripped the edge of the casket. Unfortunately, I forgot to control my enhanced werewolf strength. The coffin cracked and began to tilt. I jumped back as it tipped over with a crash that could probably be heard three counties away, my heart pounding.

Lord Chudwell's body bounced twice on the floor.

My stomach lurched when his perfectly coiffed head popped clean off on the third bounce and began rolling.

Bo pounced. "I'll get it!"

"*Nooo!*" Victoria and I yelled in unison.

The head rebounded off Bo's snout and struck Constantia's leg.

The vampire screamed and kicked it.

Our aghast gazes followed as it formed a perfect arc through the air.

Lord Chudwell's eyes snapped open mid-flight. He stared at us as his head spun comically across the parlor.

He landed amidst the vampire mourners with a fleshy thunk. More screaming ensued, the crowd scattering like startled pigeons in tuxedos, dignified composure all but abandoned. Bo took this as a challenge and bounded after the rolling head.

Victoria groaned and covered her face with her hands. "I can never show my face in society again."

"Oh, come now, you're exaggerating." Pearl smirked, tail swishing lazily. "That Husky did not disappoint."

Samuel and I dodged between the assembled vampires and went after Bo with grim determination, Barney on our heels.

The banshee funeral director started wailing, whether from distress or professional instinct I couldn't tell and hardly cared at this point. The sound set off every car alarm in the parking lot and put my wolf's teeth on edge.

"Are you getting this?" I heard Didi ask Gavin in a macabre tone tinged with delight over the shrill blaring.

"Every humiliating second," the dragon newt confirmed.

Detective Johnson was trying hard not to laugh.

Bo finally secured Lord Chudwell's head gingerly in his jaws and turned to face us, his tail wagging furiously.

His "I got the head!" came out "Gnf hrfff gnu haff!"

Lord Chudwell finally spoke.

"Excuse me, could someone please explain why I am currently staring at the back of a dog's throat?" he asked in a dignified if muffled voice. He paused. "One who appears to have had sausage for breakfast."

Barney reached Bo first and carefully extracted his friend's drool-covered head from my dog's mouth.

"Giles, you're alive." Relief colored his voice.

Lord Chudwell looked around. "Barely, by the looks of it," he remarked with impressive aplomb. "Is this my funeral?"

"Master," Betsy blubbered, rushing over. Quincy followed, chin wobbling alarmingly and the three Persian cats trailing elegantly in his wake.

"See?" Bella whispered with ghoulish pleasure to Coco and Truffles. "Totally doomed."

Gregory stormed over. "What the hell is going on, Samuel?"

My alpha sighed. "Well, Lord Chudwell is clearly not dead, Gregory."

The funeral director had managed to stop wailing and was now directing her assistants to restore some semblance of order to the no-longer-relevant proceedings. Vampires were slowly emerging from their hiding places. They whispered among themselves and shot wary looks in our direction.

An ambulance siren rose in the distance.

We got Lord Chudwell's account of the attack while the paramedics cleaned dog drool off his head and reattached it with some sort of supernatural medical tape that apparently worked better than super glue.

"There's not much to tell, really," the vampire explained. He was holding on to Mr. Snuggles while a medic worked on him. "I was in my study reviewing my investment portfolio when I heard music. Beethoven's Ninth Symphony."

"Nice tune," the paramedic muttered.

"The intruder appeared shortly after," Lord Chudwell continued. "He was a tall fellow, dressed like he'd stepped out of the 1800s. Looked vaguely familiar." The glance he shot at Barney was so quick I almost missed it. "Didn't even introduce himself before jabbing me with that syringe."

I narrowed my eyes slightly.

"Wait." Detective Johnson frowned. "You think you might recognize him in a lineup?"

Lord Chudwell shrugged and almost lost his head again. "Possibly."

I had been mulling over something for several minutes.

"Maybe that's why he took so long to recover," I told Samuel and Detective Johnson slowly. "Maybe whatever this drug the attacker is injecting his victims with delayed his revival."

"Whatever it was, it was most unpleasant," Lord

Chudwell confirmed with a shudder. "I managed to fight him off and we stumbled out into the corridor. The last thing I remember is tripping on something fluffy and falling down the stairs."

Everyone carefully scrutinized the three Persian cats.

Coco and Truffles exchanged a troubled look.

"What?" Bella asked with an innocent blink.

"It was definitely Bella," Bo hissed to Pearl.

Lord Chudwell cleared his throat. "The next thing I know, I'm waking up to this young lady's scent." He studied me curiously. "I'm allergic to powerful werewolves, you see, and your Eau de Luna is particularly strong, Miss West."

I resisted the urge to sniff myself.

"You know who I am?" I asked warily.

"Even if I didn't, your scent would have been enough to tell me who you are," Lord Chudwell said with a small smile. "It's been nearly three hundred years since I was in the presence of one as powerful as you."

I blinked. "You knew Elizabeth Rochester?"

"I had the pleasure of fighting alongside her, yes," Lord Chudwell said. "Of course, I was younger then." His expression grew misty. "Even my allergies couldn't stop me from standing beside one as strong as her."

"I'm, er, sorry about the whole head situation by the way," I said guiltily. I glanced at my dog. "Say sorry, Bo."

"I didn't mean to mess up your coiffure," Bo huffed, tail swinging.

I was about to point out that this wasn't the apology I was looking for when Lord Chudwell spoke.

"Think nothing of it. These things happen at the best funerals." The vampire chuckled. "In fact, it was quite entertaining scaring the bejeezus out of the Vampire Council."

Barney's mouth twitched.

Rita turned up just as Lord Chudwell was carefully wheeled away by paramedics, Barney in tow. The vampire had insisted on accompanying his old friend to the hospital.

"Well, this is embarrassing," the coroner said leadenly as she watched her victim leave.

"Not as embarrassing as what just happened," Detective Johnson said with a smirk. "I'll show you the video later."

I became the focus of resigned stares.

Bo plopped down on his haunches and panted noisily. "This was fun. We should do this kind of thing more often."

The last of the vampire mourners had filed out of the funeral parlor, leaving us with the Tremaines and the director.

"We apologize again for what happened, Aubrey," Gregory said stiffly.

"Yes," Victoria murmured, chagrined. "I'm terribly sorry."

"It was hardly your fault," Aubrey said with a pinched expression. "Although this will go down in history as Amberford's strangest funeral." She flashed a loaded look my way. "At least it wasn't as bad as what happened at the Holts' ball."

I swallowed a sigh, conscious today's incident had done little to help my reputation. My earpiece crackled to life, startling me.

Didi's voice came through.

"We've got movement. Tall figure in a vintage coat, behind the memorial garden."

"He's moving fast!" Gavin warned.

Samuel and I bolted toward the exit, Detective Johnson and Bo on our heels.

"Where are you going?" Gregory asked, puzzled.

"To catch our perp!" Samuel shouted.

By the time we reached the memorial garden, the figure Didi and Gavin had seen was gone. The only clue to his presence was a leather-bound volume lying in the grass.

"That's our guest book!" Aubrey exclaimed breathlessly as she arrived with the others.

"The man who's been attacking vampires is here?" Constantia asked nervously.

Detective Johnson gingerly picked up the book with a handkerchief.

Samuel frowned. "Was."

I could tell the vampire's uncanny speed worried Samuel as much as it did me.

A worried whine issued from Bo.

Even with my wolf's super senses, I could only smell a fading scent. My scalp prickled. It was just as Bella and her two companions had described it: old and dark.

Detective Johnson suddenly cursed.

"What?" I asked tensely.

"Take a look at this," the werewolf said grimly.

He showed us the guest book. It was filled with elegant signatures and condolences from today's vampire mourners. At the bottom of the last page, written in what looked and smelled suspiciously like fresh blood, were the initials "L. B."

# 15

# DARK RELATIONS

An hour later, we were back at Springhill General Hospital, this time to visit Lord Chudwell in the supernatural ward. Victoria and the Tremaines had gone home and Rita had returned to the medical examiner's office.

The vampire was sitting up in bed and looked remarkably chipper for someone who'd recently had his head reattached.

"I must say, the service here is simply marvelous," he was telling Barney when we entered his room.

"It is?" Hazel asked warily where she was attaching a blood bag to a stand.

"Indeed." Lord Chudwell beamed at the pixie. "You ladies are absolute angels. I've never felt in safer hands."

Suspicion clouded Hazel's eyes. "Do you have a concussion?"

My wolf's superhearing picked up a heated discussion at the nurses' station outside.

"Maybe he hit his head?" Hilda hissed.

"According to the paramedics, he *lost* his head," Irene corrected. "As in, it detached from his body."

"Well, whatever happened, it's a fresh change from dealing with the other lun—I mean, patients currently under our care," Joyce said firmly.

There was a brief hush.

"Should we keep this one?" Hilda suggested with a grunt. "Trade him in for Count Vlacula?"

The sound of a buzzer made the dwarf swear. "Speak of the devil."

"How about we draw straws again?" Irene asked hopefully.

"Oh, come on, I always lose at straws!" Hilda grumbled.

A faint wailing echoed across the ward.

Joyce sighed heavily. "And now it's the baron."

I focused on the conversation in the room.

Samuel had settled into one of the visitor chairs and was addressing Lord Chudwell. "How are you feeling?"

"Much better, thank you. The Type AB-negative transfusion is helping." He watched us solemnly for a moment. "Something tells me you have more questions for me."

Hazel read the room and left.

"We never asked you about the letters your butler claimed you received," I said carefully. "You know? The threats."

Lord Chudwell's expression grew shuttered. "Quincy should really mind his own business."

Detective Johnson frowned. "He was worried about you."

Lord Chudwell pursed his lips.

I pulled out my phone. "We found something at the funeral parlor. The man we believe attacked you turned up after you'd left. He left a signature in the guest book." I showed him and Barney the photo I'd taken.

Barney stared at the signature like he'd seen a ghost.

Lord Chudwell sat frozen for a moment. He finally looked at Barney.

"Barnabas," he said quietly. "You need to tell them."

The others exchanged confused looks.

My pulse quickened. I'd been right all along.

Barney knew who the perp was.

A muscle worked in the vampire's jawline. "Giles, I —" he started reluctantly.

"If he's here, in Amberford, then your friends and the vampire community need to know what they're dealing with." Lord Chudwell's voice carried surprising authority for someone's whose head had just been inside my dog's jaws. He reached over and took a gentle hold of Barney's shoulder. "You can't keep hiding from this, old friend."

The room went dead silent except for the beeping of monitoring equipment.

"You know who L. B. is?" Samuel asked Barney, his voice a mixture of hurt and shock.

Barney looked down at his fisted hands for a long moment. When he finally spoke, his voice was low and hard.

"It's Ludvik Bludworth. My great-nephew."

Samuel cursed.

Didi's eyes rounded. "Your great-nephew?!"

Gavin's nostrils started smoking.

Barney's next words lifted the hairs on the back of my neck.

"I thought—or rather I hoped—that he was long dead by now."

Bo gulped noisily in the fraught hush.

"Why would you hope your own family member was dead?" Detective Johnson asked nervously.

"Because Ludvik is—" Barney stopped, searching for the right words. "Imagine the most entitled, spoiled vampire aristocrat you've ever met. Now imagine he's also convinced he's destined to rule over all supernatural beings. That's Ludvik."

I grimaced. "So he's a giant prick?"

Samuel sighed. Lord Chudwell looked impressed.

The others gave me slightly disapproving looks.

"She's right." Barney sighed. "He's the biggest and proudest prick of them all."

Joyce, who'd been about to enter the room with a glass of water and some pills, spun smartly on her heels and retraced her steps.

Barney cast a chagrined look at the disappearing nurse.

"How long have you suspected he was the one we were looking for?" I asked cautiously.

The vampire shifted uncomfortably under our stares.

"Since the ghouls at Eternal Reserves told us about Beethoven's Ninth Symphony. It was his calling card back in the day when he was terrorizing human villages in Europe."

Didi pinched the bridge of her nose. Gavin's tail popped out.

Samuel scowled. "You should have told us, Barney. It could have prevented the other attacks!"

"No, it wouldn't have," Barney said with chilling confidence. "It's clear from the accounts we've collected these past few days that Ludvik is far more dangerous now than he was the last time I saw him. Case in point, the speed at which he's reported to move. That's unnatural, even for a vampire."

That sounded pretty bad.

"Can you tell us more about him?"

"Ludvik was always getting into trouble, even as a child." The vampire's voice turned bitter. "The society we lived in at the time didn't help. It filled his head with stupid thoughts of vampire supremacy. He was forever coming up with harebrained schemes to 'purify' the bloodlines. He constantly picked fights with werewolf cubs and refused to associate with anyone who wasn't a pureblood vampire. His parents covered for him every time, which didn't help in the long run."

"Let me guess," Detective Johnson said darkly. "Rich vampire family with too much influence?"

"You could say that," Barney muttered.

"The Bludworths were one of the most powerful vampire houses in Europe," Lord Chudwell explained calmly. "Until one of Ludvik's schemes went spectacularly wrong and almost got their entire bloodline erased from vampire royal history."

Didi sucked in air. Gavin's eyes bulged.

My mouth went dry. "You were vampire royalty?" I mumbled.

"For my sins." Barney rubbed his forehead. "Eight hundred years of watching vampire aristocracy repeat the same foolish mistakes over and over again made me leave. I came to America for some peace and quiet."

Detective Johnson stared. "Eight hundred years?!"

"Give or take some centuries," Barney said with a dismissive shrug. "Time gets a bit fuzzy after the first few hundred years."

I stared. "And you decided working for a werewolf firm in New England was your best option?" I couldn't completely mask my disbelief.

Barney sighed. "Believe me, werewolves are positively pleasant compared to vampires."

"That's true," Lord Chudwell confirmed with a nod. "They don't start wars over bloodline purity or challenge people to duels over dinner seating arrangements. More importantly, they don't stab you in the back."

"No, they just go straight for the jugular," Samuel muttered. My alpha's expression had grown increasingly grim. "What kind of scheme went wrong in Europe?" He clenched his jaw. "Does it have anything to do with what he's attempting here in Amberford?"

Barney's face grew shuttered.

"Ludvik tried to convince the vampire courts that all common-blood vampires should be eliminated," he said in a lifeless voice. "He claimed vampires who'd associated with other supernatural races were contaminated and should similarly be exterminated. My great-nephew gathered quite a following among the younger vampires."

"He was charismatic," Lord Chudwell admitted reluctantly. "Ludvik could make almost anyone believe in his cause. He convinced dozens of newborn vampires to join his movement in the old country."

My heart raced as I watched Barney. "What happened to them?"

"They died," he said flatly. "All of them. Ludvik led them into a battle they couldn't win against the vampire courts. It was a bloodbath. They attempted to overthrow the established order, after all. I'd received reports Ludvik was killed in the final battle. Those were evidently wrong."

I knew I wasn't the only one who heard the anger and pain in his voice.

The vampire must have been agonizing over the horrors his great-nephew had committed for centuries.

"If Ludvik is here, collecting and drinking blood from vampire aristocracy, then I fear he's up to his old schemes again," Barney said darkly.

"So the reason he's targeting specific bloodlines has to do with his blood purity plans?" Samuel asked stiffly.

"Yes."

I furrowed my brow. "How exactly does drinking from other vampires and taking their blood samples help his cause?"

Lord Chudwell and Barney exchanged another look.

"There were rumors," Barney said reluctantly, "about an ancient ritual that would allow a vampire to absorb the power and abilities of other bloodlines."

My stomach plummeted. "What?"

Samuel narrowed his eyes. "Absorb how?"

"By consuming their blood while they're still alive but in a comatose state," Barney replied uncomfortably. "The theory was that conscious vampires could resist the transfer, but unconscious ones couldn't."

I swallowed. "So he immobilized them not just because he needed them still?"

Bo's ears flattened.

"Your great-nephew wants to turn himself into a super-vampire?" my dog asked, tail tucked firmly between his legs.

Detective Johnson scowled. "That's impossi—!"

"Essentially, yes," Barney interrupted. "If Ludvik has found a way to make the ritual work…"

"He'll be unstoppable," Samuel concluded sourly. "And the first of a new race of vampires."

Our mate bond thrummed with tension.

"And the blood samples?" Didi scowled. "Why take those?"

"So he can experiment and further refine the process. He was quite adept at running experiments, even in those days."

Great, just what Amberford needed. A mad vampire scientist.

"What's his next move?" I asked Barney. "I'm sure you have an idea."

Barney hesitated. "He'll target another powerful vampire family to extract their blood."

Detective Johnson clenched his jaw. "Which one?"

"I'm not sure." Barney grimaced and rubbed the back of his head. "There are at least five more in Amberford that meet his criteria."

Samuel frowned at Detective Johnson. "We need to warn them. They're going to need extra security until this is over."

"Good luck with that," Barney muttered. "Vampire aristocracy doesn't respond well to being told they're in danger. They'll insist they can handle it themselves."

"Barnabas is right," Lord Chudwell said tiredly.

"Then we'll just have to—" Samuel started.

My phone rang, cutting him off. I looked at the screen and frowned.

It was Virgil.

I answered the call. "Virgil? I'm in the middle of something right now—"

"Abby!" Virgil's voice was tight with panic. "You need to get to Bean Me Up. Now!"

I froze, dread forming a leaden ball in the pit of my stomach.

"What's the matter?"

"It's Ellie." Virgil's voice cracked. "She's—she's been attacked!"

A ringing filled my ears. My vision went red.

I didn't realize I was doing something until I heard Samuel shouting.

My heart stuttered when I looked up.

Didi, Gavin, and Detective Johnson were on their

knees, their faces contorted into expressions of agony as they clutched their heads. Bo was flat on the floor, paws over his head and jaws open in a howl of pure distress. Lord Chudwell winced in bed. Barney's eyes glowed crimson where he'd jumped to his feet.

The room was shaking, the equipment was clattering wildly, my phone had cracked in my hand, and the baron was wailing even louder somewhere close by.

Samuel closed the distance to me, his expression strained and his body leaning forward as if he were fighting a storm.

"Breathe, Abby!" he yelled, his alarm finally reaching me across our bond.

I unfroze and gulped down air, a bone-deep shudder shaking me from my head to my toes. Whatever power it was I had unconsciously unleashed started to abate.

A thunk had me spinning toward the door.

Hilda had hooked the blade of her axe over the edge of the jamb and was hanging onto it grimly as she attempted to get inside the room, her nursing colleagues clinging to her legs and beard.

"What the hell was that?!" the dwarf panted.

Joyce paled when she saw me. "Oh my gosh!"

Instinct had me turning to look in the mirror above the sink.

My pulse stuttered.

My hair had gone a pure white and my eyes were glowing an amber so deep they looked like fire. Other parts of my face had taken on an uncomfortable animal appearance.

My wolf was literally under my skin and we both looked ready to murder someone.

"Abby?" Samuel laid a hesitant hand on my shoulder, as if afraid I would break.

I swallowed and clasped his fingers, his touch lending me strength to force down the rage threatening to overwhelm me.

I realized Virgil was still shouting on the line and met Samuel's worried gaze.

"Ellie's been attacked," I said in a flat voice.

My alpha swore. Bo raised his head, ears perking up and eyes round with fear.

I put my phone to my ear, my jaw set in a hard line.

"Virgil, calm down and tell me exactly what happened."

# 16
## BITTEN

THE DRIVE TO BEAN ME UP HAD NEVER FELT LONGER.

Samuel gripped the steering wheel of the Bentley so hard I was surprised it hadn't snapped. Didi was muttering what sounded suspiciously like a protection spell in the back seat. Barney stared out the window with glowing crimson eyes and an expression like thunder. Gavin's nostrils kept sparking alarmingly, to the point it was a miracle he hadn't burned down the car and us with it. Detective Johnson was squashed between the dragon newt and the vampire and looked like he was wondering what had possessed him to get inside the vehicle. Bo was pressed against the floor by my legs with his paws over his head.

He was thankfully no longer howling.

"Everyone needs to calm down," I said in a carefully controlled voice. "We don't know how bad it is yet."

"Your hands are shaking," Detective Johnson muttered.

Bo peeked at me between his toes. "He's right."

He raised his head and cautiously licked my fingers.

I stroked his head and released a tremulous breath.

Adrenaline was buzzing through my veins like I'd been zapped by lightning and my blood felt like it was on fire.

"She's been attacked by a four-hundred-year-old vampire," Barney finally said grimly. "It's bad."

Acid burned the back of my throat when I met the vampire's gaze in the rearview mirror. The rational part of my brain knew he was right, but the rest of me was too busy trying not to let my white wolf powers flatten every supernatural being within a five-mile radius to fully process his argument. I could feel them pressing against my skin like a living thing, demanding release.

The worried glances Samuel kept casting my way told me he'd never seen or felt anything like it before. I clenched my fists.

My wolf and I needed to have a serious conversation about a lot of things someday soon.

Bean Me Up's windows were dark when we pulled up outside the building. The Open sign was switched off and the door was locked.

I tried the handle anyway before knocking and calling out Virgil's name.

I could smell the vampire somewhere inside.

The door opened so fast I nearly fell forward.

Virgil's pale face appeared in the gap, his pupils aglow with a red light and his normally placid expression replaced by something that looked distinctly unhinged.

"Thank God," he breathed, opening the door wider. "She's in the back room." He swallowed convulsively. "I didn't know who else to call."

We crowded inside. Virgil stiffened a little at the sight of Barney.

Barney frowned at the younger vampire, like he was seeing something new. So could my wolf, but I was too worried about Ellie to give this more thought.

The coffee shop looked like a tornado had hit it. The tables were overturned, the espresso machine was leaking, and there were claw marks scored deep into the wooden counter.

My stomach twisted.

"What happened?" Samuel asked in a hard voice while Didi and Detective Johnson started examining the premises.

Virgil ran a shaky hand through his hair. "Like I told Abby, Ellie was practicing with the coffee machine after closing hours. It was around seven, maybe seven-fifteen?" His words came out in a rush. "I'd gone out to pick up some groceries. When I came back, there was this guy in the shop."

Barney lowered his brows. "Describe him."

"Tall, pale, expensive Victorian suit." Virgil's voice took on a bitter edge. "Ellie said he was asking about me. He wanted to know where I was and when I'd be back. Ellie told him I wasn't available."

A low growl escaped my throat.

Samuel put a restraining hand on my arm.

"Then what?" my alpha prompted.

"He said he could wait. Ordered a Type-O latte."

Virgil's laugh was hollow. "Ellie made him regular coffee with food coloring, like she always does. He took one sip of it and attacked her. That's when I walked in." He shuddered. "I've never seen a vampire move that fast. He'd grabbed her by the throat and was telling her she was an insult to proper vampiric society."

My vision started turning red around the edges. "Where is she?"

"Back room. But Abby—"

I was already moving. The others followed close behind as I pushed through the swinging doors that led to Bean Me Up's storage area.

Ellie was huddled in the corner between two large coffee bean sacks, her knees drawn up to her chest. She looked fine at first glance. Then she turned her head toward us and I saw the two puncture wounds on her neck, dark and ugly against her pale skin.

My breath locked in my throat. I felt like I'd been punched in the gut.

"Abby?" My best friend's voice was small and scared. "I think I'm in trouble."

I made myself move and was across the room in two strides and kneeling beside her. Up close, I could see she was shaking badly and her pupils were dilated.

"It's okay," I said quietly, even though nothing about this was okay. "I'm here now." I hugged her gently.

"He bit me," she whispered against my chest, as if she couldn't quite believe it. Her hands flexed reflexively in my dress. "I tried to explain that the coffee wasn't supposed to taste like actual blood, but he just kept getting madder. He said I was an affront to sacred traditions and needed to be punished."

Despite everything, I almost smiled.

Only Ellie would try to rationalize with an enraged vampire.

Bo came over and inserted his head between us with a whine. Ellie clutched his neck like a lifeline.

"How did you get away?" Barney asked quietly.

Ellie indicated the back door with a jerk of her chin. I stared.

It was hanging off its hinges.

"Virgil came back." Ellie brightened slightly. "You should have seen him, Abby. He was like a completely different person."

I followed her enthralled gaze to where Virgil hovered anxiously by the storage shelves.

"What did you do?" Detective Johnson asked warily.

"I, er—" Virgil paused and scratched his cheek, clearly embarrassed, "I may have thrown him through the door."

Surprise quickened my pulse. Samuel frowned.

Barney's eyebrows shot up. "You threw a four-hundred-year-old vampire through a reinforced steel door?"

"He was hurting Ellie," Virgil said simply.

Barney's face hardened. "It seems you've been hiding your true strength."

"I wasn't hiding it," Virgil protested. He faltered. "Okay, I was kinda hiding it. I don't want my father to know I might be one of the most powerful vampires in Amberford." He shuddered. "Can you imagine what he'd do to drag me back to the family? Besides, I don't like violence." His gaze found Ellie and his expression softened. "But nobody hurts my friends and gets away with it."

I was still wondering at the strange look in the vampire's eyes when Bo sniffed Ellie's hand and whined.

"You smell different," he told her, lowering his head.

My stomach dropped. "Different how?"

Bo's tail drooped. "Not human anymore different."

Ellie froze.

A sick realization dawned on me. I stared at the puncture wounds on my best friend's neck before twisting around and fixing Barney and Virgil with a panic-stricken stare.

"Is Ellie—?!"

"Yes," Barney confirmed grimly. "The transformation has already started."

"Our venom works quickly on humans," Virgil said uneasily.

"Transformation?" Ellie's voice climbed an octave. "What transformation? Nobody said anything about a transformation!"

Didi grimaced. Gavin and Detective Johnson exchanged an awkward glance. Samuel looked like he wanted to punch something.

I gripped Ellie's hands as she started hyperventilating.

"It's going to be okay." I swallowed heavily at the fear in my best friend's eyes and tried not to let my own dread overwhelm me. I shot another look at Barney. "How long do we have?"

"It depends on the vampire's age and power." A muscle jumped in his cheek. "Ludvik's old enough that the process should be complete within the next day or so."

"Complete into what exactly?" Ellie asked in a small voice. She'd gone deathly still.

I could tell she'd finally grasped what we were talking about.

"A vampire," Virgil said gently before I could reply. He came over and squatted beside us. "I'm sorry, Ellie. Once you've been bitten by someone of Ludvik's caliber, there's no going back."

Ellie stared at him for a long moment.

"But—I'm a vegetarian!" she finally said, horrified.

Someone snorted. I cut my eyes to Detective Johnson.

"I'm sorry," the werewolf said guiltily, sobering.

"He's right," Gavin said nervously. "I mean, whoever heard of a vegetarian vampire?"

Didi sighed. "Only in Amberford."

Virgil touched Ellie's shoulder. "I'm afraid you're gonna have to kiss your old diet goodbye. You won't be able to survive on salad alone."

Tears pooled in Ellie's eyes. She sniffed. "Even kale?"

Virgil shuddered. "Especially kale."

"Do you think I'll still be terrible at making vampire coffee?" Ellie quavered.

Detective Johnson snorted again. Samuel elbowed him viciously in the ribs.

Virgil gave the police officer a dirty look before addressing Ellie. "I wouldn't get my hopes up. You're pretty bad at making supernatural coffee in general."

I found myself appreciating the vampire's honesty.

"Great," Ellie blubbered. "Just great."

I pulled her into a hug again as she started sobbing and tried to ignore the fact that her skin already felt cooler than it should.

A thought came to my mind then. One that froze me in my tracks.

I felt a little faint as I looked at Barney and Virgil. "How much pain will she be in?"

Ellie stiffened in my hold.

Virgil bit his lip.

Barney's expression grew solemn. "It will be significant. Almost as intense as your first full moon."

My blood turned to ice. I remembered my first transformation all too well.

Ellie pulled back. Horror had widened her eyes.

"I—I don't like pain," she mumbled hoarsely.

Desperation clawed at my insides.

"There has to be something we can do," I pleaded with the others.

Their expressions told me there wasn't.

"I'm afraid she'll have to weather this on her own," Barney said firmly.

"I can give her my blood."

My head snapped to Virgil.

The vampire looked strangely determined as he faced down our shocked stares.

Barney frowned. "There's no evidence that will work. It's been attempted many times before."

Virgil jutted his chin. "There's no harm trying."

I swallowed, heart thumping hard. "You mean, giving Ellie your blood might help her through her transformation?"

"Yes." An uneasy expression flashed in Virgil's eyes. "It also means his hold on her won't be as strong."

I stilled. "His hold?"

"A newborn vampire is beholden to the one who transformed them," Virgil admitted guiltily. "They will struggle to enact their own will for some time." He looked at Ellie. "My blood may counteract that effect."

Ellie had listened to all of this with mounting horror.

"Does that mean if I don't drink your blood, I might become that—that monster's slave?!" she asked.

"Yes." Virgil hesitated. "It does mean I will hold a degree of influence over you. If you'd rather not—"

"I'll do it."

I stared at Ellie. Her eyes held a light I'd never seen before.

"I'll do it," Ellie repeated, her voice steady.

"Are you sure?" Virgil asked quietly.

Ellie nodded. "I'd rather it be you."

# 17

# TEETHING PROBLEMS

WE DECIDED TO TAKE ELLIE TO THE HAWTHORNE estate. According to Samuel, it was the safest place in Amberford right now. Even Barney agreed that the chances Ludvik would enter werewolf territory just to attack a vampire were low.

Didi and Gavin went home from Bean Me Up while Detective Johnson returned to the precinct to write up a report about today's incidents.

My shoulders unknotted when Samuel parked the Bentley outside the mansion. I hadn't realized being in our territory could bring such relief.

The pain hit Ellie when we walked through the front door.

She doubled over with a gasp. "Oh God!" She closed her eyes tightly and moaned. "It feels like my insides are on fire!"

Victoria came forward. "I have a room ready." Her voice was steady despite the unease darkening her eyes.

Pearl squinted at us as she padded next to the

Hawthorne matriarch. Hugh and Bernard hovered anxiously behind them.

Samuel had called ahead to let his family know what had happened.

A car screeched to a stop outside. Caroline and Kent stormed inside the foyer seconds later.

"We came as quickly as we could," Caroline said breathlessly.

Having the Hawthorne pack enforcers around dispelled some of my fears about our security.

A guttural sound left Ellie. Her nails sank into my skin as she tried to catch her breath against the agony storming her body, her face pale and sweat beading her forehead.

The lights in the foyer flickered.

I realized my power was responding to Ellie's distress, my wolf feeding off my fury at what had been done to my best friend.

Bo whined and backed away a couple of steps.

"Abby," Samuel warned softly.

Caroline and Kent's eyes shifted to amber, their expressions growing hyperalert as they stared at me unblinkingly, their wolves just under their skins.

"Bloody hell," Hugh muttered hoarsely.

I didn't have to look in the mirror in the hallway to know my hair and face had changed again.

Victoria's mouth tightened. "Is this what you meant?" she asked Samuel.

"Yes," my alpha said tiredly.

"Abby," Ellie whispered shakily.

I scowled at her, pain and rage warring inside me.

"It's okay." She straightened with a wince and grasped my hand with trembling fingers. "I'll be okay, so calm down."

I closed my eyes and tried to rein in the white wolf, but my anger was too strong. I ground my teeth.

Someone had hurt my best friend. They had stolen her humanity and left her to suffer through a transformation she never asked for. And I was going to make sure they paid a hefty price for their crime.

"Calm yourself, wolf."

My eyes snapped open.

Pearl was sitting in front of me, her sapphire eyes glowing with the same pale light they'd radiated at the Holts' ball.

Samuel made a worried noise and moved toward me. Victoria stopped him.

The fire in my blood slowly abated in the face of the power Pearl wielded. I could feel my wolf's hackles settling. I released a shaky breath when I finally regained control of my emotions.

Caroline and Kent relaxed a fraction.

Pearl's eyes returned to their normal color. She blinked and slowly swished her tail. "We're going to have to do something about your wolf's temper."

"How did you do that, Fur Ball?" Bo asked, wide-eyed.

"It's in the blood, Mutt," Pearl muttered.

Lines furrowed Victoria's brow as she studied me. I could tell she wanted to talk about what had just happened. She turned and led the way upstairs instead.

Virgil and I helped Ellie to the second floor.

"I have to say, this will be a first for the Hawthornes," Pearl remarked steadily as she trailed in our steps. "We've never hosted a vampire transformation before." She eyed Barney as he ascended beside her. "It's been a while since you paid us a visit, Barnabas."

"I would have preferred if it were longer," the vampire grunted.

By the time we got Ellie into bed, her skin was clammy and she was as pale as a ghost. The hairs rose on my nape when a scream left her.

She arched her back, fingers clawing desperately at the sheets.

I bit the inside of my cheek hard and shut down my wolf as best as I could.

Virgil scowled. He sat on the edge of the mattress, bit his wrist without a second's hesitation, and placed his bleeding flesh in front of Ellie's mouth.

"Drink," he ordered curtly.

The scent of the vampire's blood made my wolf grow still and had amber flaring in the depths of Samuel and Kent's pupils. Even Hugh looked alert.

Ellie blinked sweat out of her eyes. She looked at the blood pooling on Virgil's skin and shook her head in panic.

To my shock, Virgil took a mouthful of his own blood, curled a hand around the back of Ellie's head, and kissed her.

Hugh sucked in air. Victoria arched an eyebrow.

My best friend stiffened, blue eyes rounding.

"Well, that's a novel way to do things," Barney said with a frown. "Novel and stupid."

Pearl sniffed. "Ah, young love."

My pulse raced as I finally understood what had driven Virgil to defend my best friend at the risk of his own life and offer her his blood.

Ellie finally unfroze. Her hands found Virgil's shirt. She clung to him, welcoming his kiss. A shudder shook her as she finally swallowed his blood.

She wrenched her mouth free, grabbed Virgil's wrist, and started drinking with a newfound desperation.

Virgil's eyes bloomed crimson.

"We should leave," Victoria advised tactfully.

"I'm not leaving Ellie," I said mutinously.

"You will if you want to help her!" Samuel snapped. "She's about to go through a hell of a lot of pain and your power will only make this situation worse. She needs calm, Abby, not a supernatural hurricane!"

I flinched at his words. Samuel cursed and came over to hug me.

"I'm sorry," he murmured in my hair, our bond thrumming with his pain and regret. "I'm trying to help both of you."

He was right, as much as I hated to admit it.

I swallowed and looked over at Ellie.

"I'll be right outside, okay? Virgil and Barney are going to take care of you."

Ellie paused mid-suck, the action seeming to cause her pain. She looked at me from under her lashes and nodded slightly.

The last I saw of my best friend before Barney closed the door on us was the hungry look in her eyes as she feasted on Virgil's blood.

Samuel forced me to go downstairs to the sitting room.

Bernard kept a steady supply of snacks and drinks going as we spent the night waiting out Ellie's transformation. Victoria and Hugh occasionally spoke in hushed voices with Caroline and Kent while Samuel and Bo never left my side.

Pearl watched the proceedings with an almost bored expression, though even I could tell she tensed a little whenever Ellie's stifled cries of pain reached us.

It was dawn when the sounds stopped. A door opened on the second floor sometime later. Soft footsteps came from the stairs.

Barney entered the sitting room, faint circles under his eyes.

"It's over."

I rose stiffly where I'd been sitting with Samuel and Bo.

"Is—" I stopped and clenched my fists. "Is Ellie okay?"

Barney gave me a bewildered look. "She's more than okay."

# 18

# MEAT AND GREET

"GOD, I CAN'T BELIEVE I WASTED TWENTY YEARS OF MY life avoiding meat. This is incredible!" Ellie stabbed another chunk of her steak and practically moaned as she bit into it.

Bo and I studied her warily where we sat opposite her.

Caroline and Kent had gone home to their kids and the rest of us were having breakfast.

My best friend looked the picture of health as she enthusiastically devoured beef so rare I half expected it to moo.

Bo leaned over.

"Is she even chewing?" he hissed.

"I don't think so."

"I am chewing," Ellie protested, though this came out as "Gnf hrf gnuhaffhrf." Something seemed to strike her then. She swallowed and beamed, blood oozing down her chin in a thin trail. "Hey, I can hear Bo!"

"Congratulations," Pearl offered scathingly where she sat on a high chair next to Victoria. "I'm sure your life will be thoroughly enriched from the experience."

"Fur Ball, I can't help but feel that was an insult," Bo protested.

"Oh." Ellie made a face. "I can hear the kitty too. Rude much?"

Pearl hissed.

Samuel sighed and bit morosely into his toast. Victoria and Hugh were doing their best to pretend this entire situation was completely normal. Bernard looked like he needed a drink. Virgil was watching Ellie with a fond expression that did little to mask his feelings for her.

"Maybe you should slow down," Barney advised Ellie coolly as he watched her eat.

"Slow down?" Ellie narrowed her eyes while Virgil dabbed at her chin primly with a napkin. She pointed her fork at Barney. "Dude, I could eat a whole cow right now."

I blinked. I don't think I'd ever heard my best friend call anyone "dude" in my entire life.

Virgil scratched his cheek guiltily at my expression. "Yeah, about that. Ellie, er, might inherit some of my mannerisms for a while." He shifted uncomfortably under our stares.

The sight of my formerly vegetarian best friend enthusiastically devouring what appeared to be barely cooked steak for breakfast was bad enough without that little morsel of perturbing knowledge.

"Are you sure you're feeling okay?" I asked Ellie carefully.

The smell of blood was making my wolf restless, though probably not for the same reasons as Ellie's newfound enthusiasm.

My best friend nodded. "Fit as a fiddle." Her eyes brightened. "I mean, aside from the whole wanting-to-bite-people thing and the weird urge to sleep hanging upside down in a closet, I feel amazing. My senses are incredible, I think I'm stronger than I've ever been, and"—she paused, fork halfway to her mouth, and blinked at Virgil—"I'm having some very inappropriate thoughts about jumping Virgil."

My eyes bulged. Victoria choked on her bagel. Samuel looked at the ceiling and muttered something. Bernard swayed and clutched the table.

"Wow," Hugh said in a disgusted voice as he sipped his coffee.

Barney curled a lip in equal revulsion beside the werewolf.

Virgil had turned bright red. "I—that's—"

"It's not just because I drank your blood, Virgil," Ellie told the vampire in a deadly serious voice. "I mean, sure your heartbeat sounds like a lullaby and you smell really, *really* good, but I liked you even before I became a vampire."

I narrowed my eyes a little. This was news to me. But then again, I had been rather preoccupied lately.

"Really?" Virgil asked hoarsely.

Ellie nodded a little shyly. "Really."

I watched their display of mutual infatuation with

mixed feelings. Virgil was practically floating off his chair and Ellie looked like she was ready to start composing sonnets about him.

Bo seemed equally ambivalent beside me.

"I don't like this," my dog finally stated a tad sullenly. "One of you gets bitten by a werewolf and the other one is now Miss Succula. I thought my life was going to be normal."

"So did I, but here we are," I muttered.

"Normal is overrated." Pearl glowered at Ellie and Virgil with the look of someone throwing down her napkin. "Also, *must* you two be quite so demonstrative before noon? It's bad enough Abby keeps trying to drain Samuel's life force with her loins, now I have to contend with a pair of lovesick vampires under my roof."

Samuel flushed. Victoria's eyes glazed over. Hugh sighed heavily. Bernard eyed the pot of coffee like he wanted to lace it with booze and mainline its contents.

My mouth flattened to a thin line.

"I must say I'm still shocked at how well you're holding up," Barney told Ellie thoughtfully.

My best friend wrinkled her brow. "What do you mean?"

Barney waved a hand vaguely. "You have a neat appearance, you're eating with utensils instead of tearing into raw meat with your hands, and you're demonstrating a conspicuous lack of feral behavior."

Ellie stopped eating and stared. "Is that how newborn vampires usually behave?"

"Yes," Barney replied steadily. "Most newborn

vampires spend their first few weeks in a state of barely controlled bloodlust. They're typically violent, unpredictable, and completely unable to integrate into normal society. Not to mention their insane strength."

I realized I'd missed out on a lot of information last night. It was also dawning on me that Samuel had taken a huge risk bringing Ellie to the Hawthorne estate. I now understood why Victoria, Hugh, and the Hawthorne pack enforcers had looked so anxious. My chest tightened.

I knew they'd done it for me.

"Well, I feel very integrated," Ellie said firmly as she cut another piece of bloody steak.

"Maybe it's love," Bo panted.

We all stared at my dog, Ellie with her fork aloft.

"Like Virgil's pheromones are keeping her sane, somehow," Bo added, tail swinging.

"That mutt shows a surprising understanding of vampire psychophysiology," Pearl grunted.

I stared, not least because I wasn't expecting the word "psychophysiology" out of a cat's mouth. "You mean he's right?!"

Barney frowned. "It makes sense. Virgil's blood must have created a stabilizing bond that's overriding Ellie's natural newborn instincts." He glanced at me. "Your best friend is very lucky."

I wasn't sure my best friend turning into a vampire was luck, but I decided to keep that thought to myself.

Samuel sighed. "Well, at least now we can focus on the bigger problems still facing us."

His serious tone cut through the room like Ellie's knife though her steak.

"Ludvik is still out there and as dangerous as he was last night." Samuel's expression darkened. "I just hope he doesn't attack more humans."

Barney drummed his fingers on the table. "He'll only do that if he needs a reason to create chaos. Though he likely intended to kill Ellie last night, turning her into a feral newborn would have served his purpose too." He narrowed his eyes. "My great-nephew loves nothing more than a bloodbath where a lot of innocent people die as a distraction from his true goal."

A fraught hush befell us.

"What's our next move?" I asked tensely.

Samuel and Barney exchanged a look that made my stomach clench.

"We need to inform the Amberford Alliance at tonight's meeting," Samuel said reluctantly. "Gregory and Constantia have a right to know what's happening, especially since Virgil is now a target."

Virgil flinched and opened his mouth to protest.

"Samuel is right, Virgil," Victoria said firmly. "It will only make things worse if we don't tell them."

Virgil clenched his jaw.

"The other supernatural leaders need to be warned about Ludvik's scheme," Barney added.

Not only had I forgotten there was another Alliance meeting tonight, I didn't like the sound of any of this.

"We can handle it ourselves," I protested.

Samuel frowned at my bullish look. "Abby—"

"What if the Alliance decides to lock Ellie up? What

if they—" I faltered, my nails sinking into my palms. "What if they decide she's too dangerous and they sentence her to death?"

Hugh grimaced. "That's a bit melodramatic, isn't it?"

"But not untrue," Victoria said uneasily. "It has been known to happen. I've heard stories of dangerous newborns being eliminated for the greater good of the vampire community." She glanced at Barney.

I felt my temper starting to rise, along with the familiar tingle of my white wolf power. The crystal chandelier above us trembled slightly.

"Not in Amberford, but in other vampire communities," Victoria added hastily.

Barney confirmed this with a nod.

The chandelier shook some more.

Bo whined softly and nudged me with his head.

"Easy," Samuel murmured. He rose and came over, his hand finding my shoulder even as he sought to calm my emotions through the mate bond.

Ellie looked nervously around the table. "What's the Amberford Alliance?"

Victoria explained.

Ellie stared. "So these guys could really do what Abby is afraid of?" she asked uncertainly.

"Over my dead body they will," Virgil said coldly, pupils a bright crimson.

"We have to tell them eventually," Barney pointed out in a steely voice. "This isn't the kind of thing we can keep secret forever. And it's better if we control the narrative."

I chewed my lip. He wasn't wrong, but the thought

of subjecting Ellie to Alliance bureaucracy made my skin crawl.

"Fine," I agreed grudgingly. "We tell them. But on our terms and only after we've prepared Ellie for what she's going to face."

Victoria pinched the bridge of her nose. "There's less than a day left until the meeting. Will that be enough?"

Pearl swished her tail in a way that said pigs could fly first.

Ellie squirmed under our stares.

"I'll make sure she's ready," Virgil said firmly.

Ellie reached for Virgil's hand in the strained silence. He tightened his fingers around hers, his expression resolute.

My stomach churned. Maybe this was going to be the disaster I feared it would be. But watching my best friend discover happiness in the middle of this unholy mess made me care a little less about what the Alliance might do. Besides, I had new white wolf powers and I knew how to wield them. I ground my teeth as my thoughts turned to Ludvik.

That vampire had made this personal when he hurt Ellie.

And I was going to make damn sure he paid the price for what he did.

# BLOODY POLITICS

HEADING FOR THE ALLIANCE MEETING THAT EVENING felt like going to another funeral. This one with potentially more deadly drama. The usual supernatural energy that buzzed through the Chamber of Commerce felt like it had been replaced by something heavier and more ominous as we approached the building.

Or maybe that was just my fevered imagination.

"This place smells funny," Ellie said uncertainly as we approached the familiar oak doors.

She looked beautiful in a powder-blue dress from Moonlight Couture. Claudette had positively bawled when she'd seen my best friend's bone structure.

"You get used to it," Bo huffed.

"You've been here exactly once before," Samuel remarked.

"I'm a fast learner," Bo said, tail swinging.

"The Alliance members go back a long way," I explained to Ellie.

"How long?"

"Centuries," Virgil muttered. "Some of them are like pickles. Well-preserved and sour."

The Tremaine heir looked handsome but distinctly uncomfortable in a formal suit he'd borrowed from Hugh. Ellie kept looking at him like she wanted to strip him and drag him behind a car.

"Can't you control her?" Barney told Virgil coolly.

"Yes, her pheromones are making it hard to breathe," Pearl affirmed with a curled lip.

Virgil flushed.

I shot a wary look at Barney. The vampire had dropped his office-worker facade completely, his usually relaxed demeanor replaced by something far more intimidating. I could vaguely see what the vampire ladies saw in him.

The doorman who had paled at the sight of me last Friday looked positively green this time around when he saw us.

"Good evening," he managed with a gulp. "The Alliance is gathering in the *Twilight Conference Room*."

"Don't they always meet in the *Twilight Conference Room*?" I asked, trying to be friendly.

The werewolf froze like a deer in headlights.

Bo wagged his tail hesitantly. "Is that smoke coming out of his ears?"

Samuel sighed. "I think you threw him off his script."

"Sorry," I mumbled.

The doorman came back to life and gave our trio of

guests a hesitant look, like he wanted to say something. He elected to open the doors without another word.

"Did that sign say *All Species Welcome?*" Ellie asked Virgil warily as we entered the lobby.

"Yes, it did."

Ellie gave this some thought. "How many species are we talking about?"

Victoria cut her eyes to Virgil. "I thought you told her about the Amberford supernatural community?"

"I didn't have time to give her a blow-by-blow of our entire bestiary," Virgil retorted irritably.

"It is a rather long list," Pearl observed with a sniff.

Samuel's hand found the small of my back as we reached the stairs. "Remember, we're here to tell our side of the story, not to start a fight."

I could feel him trying to pacify me across the mate bond.

"I'm not making any promises," I muttered.

Victoria sighed like she needed a drink. Ellie chewed her lip worriedly. Virgil's expression had stiffened into that of someone preparing for his execution. Barney pursed his mouth in a way that indicated he would rather be swimming with alligators. Pearl appeared ready to fire someone at the smallest infraction. Bo wagged his tail with total disregard for the knife-cutting tension.

Yup, this meeting was going to be a total disaster.

Now that I'd had some time to calm down, the prospect of tonight's meeting was weighing heavily on my mind. I debated telling Samuel we should turn around, but we were already at the top of the stairs and heading down the hallway toward our doom.

Voices reached us as we approached the conference room.

"Completely unacceptable that we weren't informed immediately," someone was saying in clipped, aristocratic tones.

I recognized Wendall's voice.

"The situation was contained," came Gregory's measured, if exasperated, response through the heavy doors. "There was no immediate threat to the Alliance."

"We have company," Portia warned shrilly.

The conversation died just as Samuel pushed open the doors.

The Alliance members were already seated around the polished conference table, their expressions ranging from curious to buzzed to openly hostile. Gregory and Constantia sat at the far end, both looking like they'd aged a decade since I'd last seen them. Concern tightened their faces at the sight of their son.

A pang of sympathy shot through me. Whatever their grievance with Virgil, it was clear the couple cared for their son.

"Sorry we're late," Samuel said, even though we weren't.

Daria acknowledged this with a regal nod while we took our seats.

The rest of the Alliance members observed our group with mixed expressions. A few gazes lingered warily on Barney, while others considered Virgil and Ellie with frank disapproval.

"This is highly irregular," Oscar declared, sulfur wafting from his shadowy corner. "These meetings are for Alliance members only."

"Or their registered associates," Melody Flowers added all too sweetly from across the table. "I must say, this is quite the eclectic gathering."

"Indeed," Cornelius contributed with narrowed eyes.

Daria sighed. "How about everyone pipe down? Samuel asked for permission to bring his guests. They're here to inform us of an important matter."

I frowned at Samuel. "You told Daria?"

He shrugged. "She's the Alliance chair."

Victoria turned a cool stare on Melody. "I would have thought you'd be too busy with your little territorial disputes to attend tonight's meeting, Melody."

"Oh, I wouldn't miss this for the world, Victoria," Melody replied with a smile that could cut glass. "One must stay engaged in the community. Speaking of which, Oscar, I hear you've been expanding your reach in the neighboring towns."

Daria rolled her eyes. "Must we do this?"

Oscar bristled in his kingdom of gloom. "At least I'm doing so through legitimate means."

"Hear, hear," Portia murmured.

"Ouija boards and pamphlets advertising summoning circles are so passé, my dear," Melody said.

Her low laugh made Titania shudder.

"So is inherited snobbery," the demon shot back.

"Come now, there's no need for trash talk," Daria protested.

No one was listening to the witch.

Finnic raised a drinking horn half his size. "How about we get this show on the road? I have places to be and barrels to drink." The dwarf's voice had an edge to it that said his battleaxe may soon make an appearance.

"How about *you* try not to drink at every damn meeting?" Wendall snapped, his nostrils sparking with irritation.

"It's Friday," Finnic growled, as if that explained everything.

"You lot are giving the Alliance a bad rep," Cornelius said icily.

Titania bobbed her head, gossamer wings fluttering agitatedly.

"He's not wrong," Portia contributed with a sniff.

"Indeed," Pearl sneered.

"Word," Bo muttered.

"The next one who interrupts is going to be saying 'ribbit' for the rest of the weekend!" Daria snarled.

The speed at which the room fell silent indicated she had made true on this threat in the past.

"Are these really the most powerful people in Amberford?" Ellie whispered doubtfully to Virgil.

I could see why my best friend would think this. Trying to deal with the Alliance felt a bit like trying to herd a roomful of cats, most of them snooty Persians.

Daria rubbed her temples. "Samuel, you raised this emergency agenda item. The floor is yours."

Samuel stood and waited until he had everyone's attention before addressing the room.

"You've all probably heard the rumors about what's been happening in Amberford this week. The blood bank robberies Gregory reported to us at our last meeting in fact escalated and he rightly assigned Hawthorne & Associates to carry out an investigation into the matter."

"He just told us about it." Wendall flashed a dark look at Gregory.

"You could have sent a text on the group chat, Gregory," Portia complained.

"If he's anything like Samuel, he probably deleted the group chat," Pearl said nastily.

Guilt danced briefly in Samuel's eyes. Gregory's face tightened.

Finnic raised an eyebrow. "So it wasn't just a newborn fledgling?"

"No. And things have taken a bad turn since. Several prominent vampires have also become the victims of the perpetrator." Samuel frowned. "We almost lost Lord Chudwell on Wednesday."

"I heard about that funeral," Titania said.

I earned some wary looks from the Alliance as they began talking animatedly.

Daria scowled, magic bursting into life in her right hand.

The noise died down abruptly.

"That's so cool," Ellie mumbled.

Even Pearl looked impressed.

"The affected vampires are currently recuperating

at Springhill General," Samuel continued smoothly once Daria put away her magic. "Unfortunately, events escalated once more yesterday."

Cornelius grimaced. "You mean, this gets worse?"

"Yes. A human was bitten and turned into a vampire by the same perpetrator."

The Tremaines froze. Titania gasped. Melody stilled. Daria's eyes shrank to slits. Portia made a sound that caused the chandelier to vibrate and put my teeth on edge.

The other Alliance members shifted uneasily in their seats.

"The victim was Ellie Martin," Samuel continued, indicating my best friend. "She was targeted because the attacker was looking for Virgil."

Constantia unfroze and shot to her feet. "What?" She turned to her son, her pupils a bright red. "Are you alright?!"

"Yes, Mother." A guilty note crept into Virgil's voice.

Constantia swallowed and hesitated before sitting down stiffly.

"You brought a newly turned vampire to an Alliance meeting?" Melody asked in a voice that could have turned lava to ice.

Several Alliance members were looking at Ellie like she had rabies. Portia moved her chair away slightly.

My shoulders knotted at the tension thickening the air.

Barney flashed me a warning look.

"Miss Martin is stable," he told the Alliance

dismissively. "The fact that she hasn't ripped out any of your throats yet is proof of that."

"That's not funny, Barnabas," Titania huffed.

Daria seemed in half a mind to agree.

"I could really do that?" Ellie whispered warily to me and Virgil. "Rip their throats out?!"

I made a face. "Probably."

"Definitely," Virgil affirmed, a steely glint in his eyes. "Let me know if you get the urge and I'll tell you who to go for first."

Ellie, Pearl, Bo, and I gave Virgil an admiring look.

"Why my son?" Gregory asked. His voice carried more dread than anger.

"Because Virgil's blood is something Ludvik Bludworth won't be able to resist," Barney said in a deadly tone.

# 20

# FULL DISCLOSURE

THE BLOOD DRAINED FROM CONSTANTIA'S FACE. "Ludvik? You mean *that* Ludvik?!"

Gregory had gone similarly ashen-faced beside his wife.

Cornelius's face tightened. "Even I've heard of him."

"Your great-nephew?" Lines marred Melody's delicate brow.

"That's who the perpetrator is?!" Titania asked, aghast.

It seemed Ludvik's reputation preceded him.

"Yes," Barney said flatly. "As a few of you know, my great-nephew is a four-hundred-year-old vampire with a history of attempting to overthrow vampire courts in Europe. He's specially obsessed with purifying vampire bloodlines."

"We received a blood purity manifesto," Gregory confirmed.

Constantia removed the letter from her bag and passed it to Daria.

Portia and Titania leaned over to read it.

Wendall narrowed his eyes at Barney. "You want us to believe it's a complete coincidence that this great-nephew of yours is here, causing havoc in Amberford?"

"If you're implying he followed me here, you would be wrong," Barney said coldly. "I had long presumed Ludvik dead. There is no love lost between us. That he ended up in the same town as me after all these centuries is a twist of fate even I didn't see coming."

"What does this Ludvik guy want?" Finnic grunted.

"To make this town his ultimate experiment."

Confusion washed across the faces of the Alliance members.

Barney sighed. "He's targeting vampire aristocracy so he can collect their blood and use an ancient ritual to absorb their powers. This would theoretically make him the first of a new pureblood vampire race. One powerful enough to do what he's always wanted: eliminate vampires of common blood and rule over other supernatural communities."

Finnic scowled. "So a new Vampire Lord? Like the good old days?"

Barney nodded grimly. "Exactly."

The room erupted.

"Impossible!" Oscar scoffed.

"That's just a myth," Wendall protested.

Cornelius frowned heavily. "Rituals with that kind of power were destroyed centuries ago."

"I agree," Melody said tightly. There was a hard glint in the fae witch's eyes.

"They're right," Portia keened, her hair unraveling in her agitation.

Daria and Titania exchanged a troubled look.

"*Enough!*" Gregory's voice cut through the noise like a blade. The vampire's eyes were crimson with fury. "If Barnabas and Samuel believe the threat is real, then we must treat it as such!"

"Thank you, Gregory," Barney said quietly as the echoes died down.

"Don't thank me yet," Gregory replied coldly. He shot a look at Virgil, his expression growing conflicted. "You said my son was targeted because of his blood. What did you mean by that?"

"Ludvik must have found out Virgil is from one of the purest vampire lineages in New England." Barney hesitated. "But it wasn't just for that reason. He could probably tell how powerful Virgil was from his scent."

Constantia and Gregory stared at Barney like he'd lost his mind.

Virgil glowered accusingly at the older vampire. "I'm pretty sure I asked you not to reveal that."

"This matter is too important not to have all our cards on the table," Barney retorted.

"Barney is right, Virgil," Samuel said.

"Powerful?" Constantia repeated. "My son?"

Gregory looked equally confused. "But—Virgil failed the vampire trials."

I stared before leaning sideways toward Victoria.

"There are vampire trials?" I hissed out the corner of my mouth.

"Yes, to determine who can be the next head of a family, among other things," she murmured.

This was news to me.

Ellie gulped. Bo's eyes brightened with unhealthy interest.

Everyone else was looking at Virgil.

"He threw Ludvik through a steel door," Barney explained. "Even I might struggle in a fight with your son," he told the Tremaines.

Surprise flashed across Virgil's face.

His parents sat shell-shocked across the way.

Gregory finally recovered and pinned his son with a hard stare. "What happened at the vampire trials?"

Virgil rubbed the back of his neck awkwardly. "I deliberately flunked them."

"What?!" Constantia squealed. "But—why?!"

"Because I don't want to step into Father's shoes and be made to continue the old traditions!" Virgil snapped.

Constantia recoiled. Gregory swallowed hard and laid a hand on her arm.

I felt a little sorry for them.

"Virgil, you shouldn't upset your parents like that," Ellie admonished softly.

"She's right," Victoria said kindly.

Virgil clenched his jaw.

"Do you hate our family that much?" Gregory asked his son in a haunted voice.

Virgil blew out a frustrated sigh. "I don't hate our family. I hate that the vampire community we're supposed to lead doesn't want to change. I hate that *you* won't allow me to try and change it."

"The bloodsuckers could do with being dragged kicking and screaming into the twenty-first century," Finnic grunted before taking a swig of his drink.

"Must you call them that?" Daria asked sharply. "And how much have you had to drink?"

"I mean, Finnic's not wrong, and neither is Virgil," Titania said uneasily while Daria and the dwarf had a tense exchange about the legal alcohol limit for attending an Alliance meeting. "Some vampire families still use hearses for transportation."

I made a face. The mystery of why Amberford had so many hearses was finally solved.

Gregory's jaw set in a rigid line, but not before I glimpsed the hurt in his eyes.

"I wished you'd told me that instead of leaving our home," he told Virgil half-accusingly.

"You never had time for me," Virgil protested.

"Virgil," Constantia said gently. "You're our son. We'll always have time for you."

Virgil flushed, his chin trembling.

Titania sniffed and dabbed at her eyes with a hanky.

"So why did Miss Martin get bitten?" Daria asked. The witch looked uncomfortable at all the public displays of affection taking place in the *Twilight Conference Room.*

"When Ludvik couldn't find Virgil at Bean Me Up, he took his frustration out on Ellie," I said.

I decided not to mention my best friend's appalling

skills at coffee making had probably triggered the episode of violence.

Cornelius's puzzled gaze swung between me and Ellie.

"Do you two know each other?"

"We live together," I said. "Ellie is my best friend."

Ellie beamed.

Daria's face fell. "Ah."

"What an unlucky coincidence," Melody remarked thoughtfully. "That both of you got bitten within a month of each other."

Portia frowned. "Almost like it was fate."

I couldn't deny that it was a freaky situation to be in.

"Still, it doesn't explain why Miss Martin is not acting like a normal newborn," Gregory said.

"That's because Virgil gave me his blood," Ellie said cheerfully. "It was delicious."

The Alliance members stared at her like she'd just suggested a full-on orgy.

"I thought that was just an urban legend," Oscar said warily.

"So did I," Wendall muttered.

"You gave her your blood?!" Constantia asked, stunned.

Virgil's face tightened. "It was the only thing I could think of to help Ellie through her transformation."

"But—why go so far for a perfect stranger?" Cornelius asked.

Virgil and Ellie exchanged a hesitant look.

Gregory lowered his brows, understanding dawning on his face. "Wait. Don't tell me—"

"Ellie and I like each other," Virgil declared. He jutted his chin and took Ellie's hand.

Ellie smiled mistily.

Gregory looked like he was considering turning to religion.

Constantia swayed.

Titania supported her with her hands and murmured words of reassurance while giving Portia and Daria a glance that said they were gossiping about this over cocktails later.

"Virgil's blood stabilized Ellie," Barney said. "His emotions for her likely influenced her transformation."

Wendall's face twisted in disgust. "Like a love potion?"

Pearl wrinkled her face like she was ready to cough up a fur ball.

"Love potion, chemistry, whatever it was, it worked," Samuel said curtly.

Melody fixed Ellie with an intense stare. "How fascinating. Maybe we should study this in more detail."

"She's not a circus attraction." Virgil's eyes flashed crimson.

A low growl left my throat, unbidden. "What he said."

"Abby and Virgil are right." Gregory had recovered from his shock and was studying his son and Ellie with a frown. "Miss Martin is now our family's responsibility. We are duty bound to offer her our protection."

Surprise flared on Virgil's face. "You're not disappointed?"

Gregory sighed. "You did what you thought was best under the circumstances, son. And I know you wouldn't have taken that decision lightly."

Everyone startled when Pearl jumped on the table.

"Maybe we should get on with the purpose of this meeting," the cat said with an imperious swish of her tail. "Like the homicidal vampire trying to overthrow Amberford's supernatural society."

There was a general clearing of throats.

"Pearl's right," Samuel said. "I want to put a motion forward to focus Alliance resources on finding and stopping Ludvik."

"Before he completes his ritual," Barney murmured.

"Seconded," Gregory said immediately.

"Hold on," Wendall interjected. "Are we seriously considering deploying Alliance resources based on some wild speculation? We don't even know where this Ludvik character is hiding."

"What seems reckless is ignoring a credible threat," Finnic said, scowling. "If this bloodsucker is half as dangerous as Barney says he is, we need to stop him."

"I agree," Titania added. "The risk is too great to ignore."

Portia nodded.

"This sets a dangerous precedent," Cornelius warned.

Daria's mouth flattened to a thin line. "Motion on

the floor. All in favor of allocating Alliance resources to tracking and stopping Ludvik Bludworth?"

Samuel, Victoria, Gregory, and Constantia's hands shot up immediately, followed by Daria's, Titania's, and Portia's. Finnic raised his tankard. Cornelius sighed and nodded.

Bo raised a paw.

Oscar scowled. "We told you that you weren't a member of the Alliance."

"Losers weepers," my dog huffed.

"That means you're getting him whether you like it or not," Pearl translated nastily.

I sighed at the frosty looks and frowns from the Alliance.

"He's a lovable doofus once you get to know him."

"Moving on," Daria said briskly. "This is a formality, but I need to ask for the records. Anyone opposed to the motion?"

Wendall and Oscar raised their hands.

"Duly noted," Daria muttered under her breath as she took notes. "The lizard and the demon are chickens."

"Hey!" Oscar protested.

Daria ignored him. "Abstaining?"

Ellie's hand shot up.

"I think this is too much responsibility for a new vampire," my best friend said bravely in the faces of everyone's leaden stare.

Oscar's territory of darkness expanded by a couple of feet. Wendall's nostrils sparked like the Fourth of July.

I grabbed Ellie's hand and put it down quickly.

Daria sighed. "Motion carries, eight to two."

"This is a mistake," Wendall muttered.

"The only mistake would be doing nothing," Gregory said firmly.

The meeting ended after everyone was assigned their roles. Hawthorne & Associates was left in charge of coordinating the search for Ludvik with Barney and Gregory's assistance, while the rest of the Alliance was tasked with getting their communities ready for a possible battle.

Gregory and Constantia pulled Virgil to the side when the Alliance members began to file out. Constantia hugged her son and spoke to him in a low voice. Virgil nodded, his expression softening. Gregory patted his back awkwardly.

"Come on, we should give them some space," I told Ellie quietly.

Bo whined. I realized my best friend was still sitting in her chair.

Her eyes had taken on a distant, unfocused quality.

The hairs rose on the back of my neck. "Ellie?"

Samuel tensed at my tone. He and Barney approached from where they were talking with Daria, Victoria and Pearl trailing in their wake.

Ellie blinked, seeming to come back to herself. Confusion clouded her face as she looked at me.

"Abby?"

My pulse quickened. "What's wrong?"

"I think I just had a…vision," she mumbled.

# 21

# PREMIUM RESERVE

"This is worse than watching paint dry," Bo grumbled from his position near the van's back doors.

"No one told you to come," Samuel said pointedly.

"What, and leave Abby alone with you?" Bo huffed indignantly. "You should thank your lucky stars I'm here, protecting your wolfy virtue."

Detective Johnson snickered. My mouth pressed to a thin line.

"Pearl put you up to this, didn't she?" I asked my dog coolly.

"Don't involve the cat," Bo sniffed. "Or her jerky bribe."

"Tell me again why we're sitting outside a blood bank at seven in the morning on a Saturday?" Didi groaned. "I haven't had enough coffee yet for this level of suffering."

"Because Ellie's vision showed Ludvik was looking at a notebook with this address in it," I explained patiently for what felt like the hundredth time. "Since

Hemoglobin Haven caters to vampire aristocracy, he's probably planning to hit it today."

We'd been watching Amberford's most exclusive boutique blood bank since dawn. The upscale establishment was located in the ritzy Maple Park district, next to Temple Heights. It had valet parking and an ice sculpture of a bat in the waiting room.

No one had been more surprised than me when Ellie had revealed what she'd seen last night. She hadn't exactly been happy about having some weird mental link to the vampire who'd tried to kill her but had done her best to describe the details of her vision.

The whole psychic-vampire-bond thing was new to Barney.

I tried to find a comfortable position in the cramped surveillance van. Seeing as it currently contained three werewolves, a vampire, a witch, a dragon newt, and a sulking Husky, this proved impossible.

"I can't believe we're working Saturday overtime," Gavin muttered, peering through the viewfinder of his camera. Smoke curled from his nostrils.

Didi cut her eyes to Samuel. "I hope we're getting premium pay for this."

"Yes, I'm paying you guys extra," Samuel said testily. "So how about everyone put a sock in it?"

"Lucky you," Detective Johnson muttered, unwrapping an egg and bacon bagel. "I don't get overtime pay."

He clocked Bo's focused stare and guarded his food closely.

Samuel's answer satisfied Didi for all of five seconds. She pursed her lips. "You know, it's weird having you on a stakeout with us."

Samuel frowned. "Why?"

"It's like trying to have sex in front of your teacher. Awkward, painful, and liable to bring the law down on you."

Detective Johnson choked on his bagel. Samuel rubbed his temples.

I had to agree with Didi. Since Virgil had gone home to reconcile with his parents, I'd spent last night at my apartment with Ellie. Having Samuel in a confined space this morning was testing the limits of my self-control, especially this close to my next full-moon transformation. The fact that he was wearing casual clothes that showcased his muscular physique wasn't helping.

I swallowed a sigh, hating that Pearl had been right.

There was a crumpling noise. We all looked at Barney.

The vampire was reading a newspaper and sipping a cup of blood orange tea like he was in the drawing room of his home. He became conscious of our stares.

"What?"

"You realize we're on a stakeout, right?" Detective Johnson asked.

"Yes, and I'm all ears and nose," Barney replied.

Didi curled a lip at that.

A crackling sound came from the radio. "Team Alpha, this is Base. Do you copy?"

Samuel picked up the handset. "We copy, Nigel. Also, I'm pretty sure I told you not to call us that."

"But Team Alpha is such a cool name," the boogeyman protested.

"It is a cool name," Gavin concurred.

Bo huffed an agreement. Detective Johnson dipped his head.

Even I had to concede it had a ring to it.

Samuel sighed. "Any activity on the street cameras?"

"Negative." Nigel hesitated. "Though I should mention, the system's been acting up all morning. I keep getting these weird glitches."

I tensed and exchanged a cautious glance with the others.

"Define glitches," Samuel said stiffly.

"It's hard to describe. It's like something's interfering with the signal, but only intermittently."

Didi arched an eyebrow. "It could just be technology failing us."

"Or it could be our perp," Detective Johnson said, frowning.

Samuel's expression hardened. "Try and look into those glitches," he instructed Nigel. "And if any of the cameras go dark, let us know ASAP."

"Okay. Oh and Mindy wanted me to tell you she's excited about her first field mission."

Though we'd all had doubts on this subject, Barney had suggested bringing Mindy along since ghosts didn't have a scent that vampires could detect. She was supposed to be our invisible advance scout.

"Where is she now?" Samuel asked warily.

"Inside the blood bank. She's been possessing their security system for the past thirty minutes."

That didn't sound good. We traded another round of wary glances.

"Please tell me she's not rearranging their filing system," Didi said sharply.

Nigel's silence was laced with guilt. "I'll get back to you on that."

There was a longer pause. The boogeyman came back online.

"She's reorganized their appointment system by blood type and vintage," he confessed sheepishly.

Didi cursed. "That damn ghost!"

Barney frowned. "I hope she didn't mess with their inventory. That could lead to allergic reactions."

I briefly wondered what an allergic reaction might look like on a vampire, before deciding it was too early to picture that stomach-churning possibility.

"She only color-coded it," Nigel protested weakly. "The staff think it's a Christmas miracle."

"Jesus," Detective Johnson muttered.

Bo stretched and yawned. "How much longer do we have to sit here?"

"However long it takes," Samuel said between gritted teeth.

"But I'm bored," Bo whined. "And hungry. And this van smells like Gavin's lunch."

I sighed.

"What's wrong with my lunch?" Gavin asked defensively.

"It's got tentacles in it," Bo said with a shudder.

"Calamari is perfectly normal," Gavin protested.

"For humans, maybe," Bo muttered.

"You eat kibble," Gavin pointed out.

"Kibble doesn't have suction cups."

"Will you two keep it down?" Samuel snapped. "We're supposed to be conducting a covert surveillance."

Bo huffed sullenly.

Gavin went back to his camera but kept glancing at his lunch bag with wounded pride.

The radio crackled again.

"Base to Team—I mean, this is Base. Mindy's reporting movement inside the blood bank," Nigel said. "A well-dressed customer just entered the building. He's wearing an expensive suit and talking like he owns the place."

"That could be any vampire aristocrat," Barney remarked.

"Here, I'll get Mindy to send us a visual."

The monitor in the van came to life.

"Hello," someone whispered loudly amidst the static.

We all screamed a little.

"Is that you, Mindy?" I mumbled, clutching my chest.

"Yes," Mindy replied. "I'm in the system." The ghost sounded pleased with herself. "Would you like me to describe the atmosphere?"

"No, thanks," Samuel said hastily. "We just want to focus on that customer. Can you show us?"

"Oh." Mindy sounded disappointed. "That sounds a

bit boring, but you're the boss."

Samuel squeezed his eyes shut and muttered something under his breath.

Detective Johnson made a sympathetic sound and patted his shoulder.

The monitor switched to the view of a security camera in the foyer. We stared at a familiar-looking figure.

"Isn't that Count de Vile?" Gavin asked suspiciously.

"What the hell is he doing here?" Samuel snapped.

"Being a pain in the ass by the looks of it," I observed.

The reception staff were having a hard time dealing with the count.

"He must have self-discharged from the hospital," Didi muttered.

"I bet Hilda and Hazel are celebrating," Bo panted.

Samuel scowled. "Ludwik might leave if he sees him. Didi and Gavin, go inside and see if you can get him out of there. The rest of us will get in position."

Didi and Gavin exited the van with unenthusiastic expressions. They tried their best to look like a witch and dragon newt in need of specialty blood products as they headed for the front entrance.

"I still think I should go with you," Bo protested as Samuel, Barney, and I got ready to head out to cover the back exit.

He was staying in the van with Detective Johnson to serve as our lookout.

"Dogs aren't allowed inside blood banks," I told him for the third time.

"What about service dogs?"

"You hate being a service dog."

"I could be for once," Bo huffed. "A very helpful one, in fact."

I narrowed my eyes. "You tried to eat evidence during our last stakeout."

"It was shaped like a bone," Bo said defensively.

"It was a femur."

"Exactly. Bone-shaped."

"Wow," Detective Johnson muttered.

Samuel pinched the bridge of his nose. "Nigel, you copying?"

"Loud and clear. The Husky is a liability."

"Not that." Samuel sighed. "Tell Mindy to stay alert. And keep monitoring things closely from your end."

"Oh. Gotcha."

Samuel, Barney, and I left the vehicle and circled around to the back. We were halfway there when Nigel's voice crackled in our earpieces.

"Mindy's reporting a problem."

Samuel's shoulders knotted. "What kind of problem?"

"She accidentally triggered the fire suppression system," Nigel said apologetically. "The customers are evacuating."

"Any sign of our target?" I asked while Samuel cursed softly.

Didi's mildly disgusted voice came through the comm before Nigel could reply.

"People are leaving en masse. Wait, Gavin, watch where you're—!"

A loud crash echoed through the earpiece. It was following by an intense sizzling sound.

"I hope you guys have stakeout insurance," Detective Johnson said flatly.

"Why?" Samuel groaned.

"Because the dragon newt just slipped on the floor, crashed into the ice sculpture, and melted it in his panic."

"The bat one?" I said warily.

"Yup. It's more of a puddle now."

"This is going well," Barney remarked with a pinched expression.

"FYI, the Husky says this wouldn't have happened if they'd taken him as a service dog," Detective Johnson added.

I narrowed my eyes.

"Uh-oh." Nigel's tone had grown urgent. "Mindy's just lost contact with the security system. Something's fighting her for control."

My pulse spiked.

"Fighting her how?" Tension knotted Samuel's shoulders.

"She says it feels like another presence in the system. Something old and angry."

"We should get in there," I told Samuel and Barney urgently.

They nodded. We moved toward the rear exit.

Nigel's voice was full of dread when he spoke again. "The cameras just went dark."

My blood ran cold. "All of them?"

"Every single one," Nigel confirmed grimly.

"Nigel, tell Mindy to get out of there," Samuel ordered sharply. "Didi, Gavin, evacuate the staff and the customers. I don't care what excuse you give them, just get them out!"

I grabbed the back door of Hemoglobin Haven. It was locked. I let my wolf slip effortlessly under my skin and yanked sharply on the handle.

The door ripped out of the wall like it was made of paper.

Samuel and Barney stared at the crumbling bricks surrounding the gaping opening.

I grimaced. "Sorry."

I dropped the door and ran inside with them.

# 22

# FAMILY REUNION

THE BACK OF THE BLOOD BANK WAS A MAZE OF STERILE corridors and fluorescent lighting. Alarms started blaring as we raced down them, the red lights casting an ominous glow across the wet floor and walls.

"Mindy managed to regain control of the security system!" Nigel yelled in our earpieces.

The sprinklers stopped just as we reached a junction.

"This way," Barney said tensely. He turned left.

Samuel and I followed him.

The vampire slowed as we approached a set of double doors.

"The main cold storage is through here. If Ludvik's after premium blood, this is where he'll be headed."

I frowned. "How do you know that?"

"Because I've been here before," the vampire said grimly. "And even you should be able to smell the blood bags from here."

I made a face as my wolf picked up a veritable

buffet of scents coming from the cold storage. A brouhaha rose from the front of the building. Didi's sharp tone cut through the raised voices.

"And I'm telling you people you need to leave. Now!"

"This is most irregular," Count de Vile protested shrilly.

Several other voices joined in, each sounding as pompous as the others.

"You can complain to management afterward," the witch snapped. "Now, I suggest you vamoose before you get accidentally fried by an excited dragon newt."

"Yeah," Gavin groused. "I have sparks and I'm not afraid to use them!"

Detective Johnson suddenly cursed in our earpieces.

Samuel's shoulders knotted. "What is it?"

"Something just flew past the van. I couldn't catch a good look!"

I heard Bo barking in the earpiece and met Samuel's amber gaze, my heart racing. "It's him!"

The lights flickered.

A cry from the direction of the reception area had us whirling around.

Didi cursed in the distance. Gavin yelped.

The hairs rose on the back of my neck. Something was coming.

A low growl left Samuel as he prepared to transform. Crimson filled Barney's pupils, the vampire growing a foot in height. I'd barely loosened my hold on my wolf when a figure flashed around a corner and barreled toward us.

I caught a glimpse of hungry red eyes and sharp fangs before it slammed into me and sent me crashing through the double doors into the storage area.

"Abby!" Samuel shouted, the word an alarmed half growl.

I landed on my back with a grunt. My eyes widened.

I rolled and narrowly missed the claws headed for my eyes, my breath misting in front of my face in the icy room.

The vampire lunged at me with inhuman speed.

The transformation hit me hard and fast. My bones lengthened, my muscles expanded, and my senses exploded as my wolf emerged under the flickering lights.

My world shifted into a myriad of colors, scents, and sounds.

Ludvik's eyes blazed with an unholy light as he approached, his features etched sharply across my enhanced vision and his heartbeat anything but steady in my ears.

I could smell his fear. His rage. And something else —something old and rotten that clung to the vampire like expensive cologne gone bad and made my stomach roil.

I missed his attack by a hairbreadth, raked his chest with my claws as I leapt, and landed behind him with a solid thud.

Samuel's black wolf joined me, the anger

thrumming through our mate bond reflected in his glowing eyes and his vicious snarl.

*Are you okay?!*

I nudged him with a shoulder. *Yes.*

Barney flanked my other side, his face tight.

Ludvik straightened and stared at us with an ugly expression. He was tall and lean like Barney, with sharp cheekbones and the kind of eyes that suggested he'd outlived everyone he'd ever cared about. His dark hair was perfectly styled and his clothes immaculate but for the damage my claws had inflicted.

I lowered my head and growled when he touched the blood I had drawn and licked his fingers.

"What a waste." A cold light suffused Ludvik's crimson gaze as he studied Barney. "Uncle Barnabas, you haven't changed one bit since I last saw you. Where was it again?" His mouth twisted mockingly. "Oh yes. The Austrian vampire court. If I remember correctly, you tucked your tail between your legs and disappeared like the obedient dog that you are the moment you were instructed to do so."

Barney ignored the insult and narrowed his eyes. "You, on the other hand, have changed a lot, dear nephew."

My wolf stirred uneasily at the undercurrent of dread in Barney's voice.

Ludvik smelled wrong for a whole lot of reasons I didn't understand. Even Samuel watched the vampire with a wary look, like he couldn't make out what he was exactly.

I tensed when Ludvik's gaze found me.

"So this is Amberford's famous white wolf. You are not quite what I expected." Disdain underscored his words.

My hackles rose. I bared my fangs with a feral sound, muscles bunching.

Ludvik's laughter was cold and empty.

"How refreshingly direct. That's about the only thing I ever liked about you dogs." He paused and smirked. "I must say, your friend's transformation was highly disappointing. I had hoped she would provide a suitable distraction."

I froze.

"A feral newborn vampire tearing through Amberford's human population would have been perfect cover for my work," Ludvik continued in a slightly bored voice. "Especially the best friend of Amberford's new hero. Instead, I hear the girl's been…*domesticated*. And by that Tremaine boy, no less."

Fury surged through my veins, a hot feeling that electrified every cell in my body. The bastard had known exactly who Ellie was when he'd targeted Bean Me Up.

Barney took a step forward before I could leap for Ludvik's throat.

"Stop this madness, Ludvik," he said coldly. "Your plan will never work. You cannot take on the whole of Amberford, let alone the clans of New England."

"Oh, I think you would be surprised at what I can do, Uncle," Ludvik said in a brittle voice. "And I fully intend to put things back the way they should be, this time around. Vampires ruling." His gaze flitted to me and Samuel. "And lesser creatures knowing their place."

I moved.

*Abby!* Samuel shouted. He cursed and bounded after me.

By then, I'd closed the distance to Ludvik. My belly clenched when he blurred out of view. I skidded through the space where he should have been and slammed side-first into a shelf.

Metal caved under the impact.

Samuel hunkered over me as boxes rained down on us.

We shook ourselves free and looked around.

Ludvik was nowhere to be seen.

There was movement out the corner of my wolf's eye. My head snapped around.

Barney was moving in a way I'd never seen the vampire move before.

He practically levitated off the ground as he leapt, his face locked in a furious expression and his crimson gaze focused on something above us.

My blood ran cold when I followed his gaze.

Ludvik was upside down and clinging to the ceiling, the vampire's face a rictus of rage.

He blurred again, his outline edged by thin dark trails. Barney snarled, his claws missing Ludvik by an inch.

A grunt suddenly left Samuel. A flash of pain echoed brightly across our bond. I realized he was bleeding and whimpered.

Ludvik had cut his leg.

The vampire flitted like a shadow around us as we regrouped in the middle of the room, his attacks faster than anything I'd ever faced. He punched Barney in the solar plexus and sent him smashing into a wall. Blood sprayed from the vampire's lips as he dented the plasterwork with his back.

I barely managed to block Ludvik when he came for Samuel again. His blow caught my shoulder and sent me spinning me across the floor. Pain flared through my left rib cage when I crashed violently into a metal cabinet. My werewolf healing kicked in.

Samuel slipped out of the way of Ludvik's claws with a snarl, feinted to one side, then struck on the other, his jaws finding a slim gap in the vampire's defenses.

Ludvik hissed in pain when the black wolf caught his wrist with his fangs. He backhanded Samuel across the face.

I watched in horror as the force of the blow sent my alpha flying into a row of shelves. He landed hard on the floor. I was beside him in a single leap and kept him at my back as I turned to face his attacker, my hackles trembling and my wolf ready to shred the bastard to pieces.

There was movement behind Ludvik. I lunged, Barney coordinating his attack with mine.

He vanished before our eyes again.

Barney swore as we crashed into each other and plummeted to the ground in a tangle of limbs.

The double doors clattered open.

I looked around where I'd cushioned Barney's fall.

Ludvik was making his escape with several blood bags, his form leaving a faint shadowy imprint in the air.

I wriggled free and gave chase, Barney and Samuel scrambling to catch up.

Cries erupted as we dashed out into the reception, the ghoul staff falling back in panic at our sight. By the time we got outside, there was no trace left of Ludvik.

Samuel and I stopped beside Barney on the road and shifted back to our human forms.

"Where the hell did he go?!" I snarled, heart pounding and breaths coming hard and fast.

"I don't know," Barney replied grimly.

Samuel spun on himself and searched the skies. He stiffened. "There!"

We followed his gaze as he pointed to the south.

A shrinking flock of bats was etched starkly against the pale clouds.

I scowled at Barney. "Is it normal for a vampire to move like that?"

"No," he replied, his voice a mix of anger and dread. "I have never witnessed that kind of speed in a member of our race. Not even the Lords of the Old Country."

This wasn't the kind of news I needed to hear right now. Samuel and I exchanged a tense look.

We were in over our heads and we all knew it.

Footsteps pounded on the road. Didi and Gavin were running toward us, Detective Johnson following closely.

"You should do something about your leg," Barney told Samuel.

My chest tightened when I saw the ugly wound on my alpha's thigh, the fresh scent of his blood tickling my nostrils.

"It'll heal in no time," he reassured at my expression.

I clenched my jaw harder.

The others reached us.

"We got all the customers out," Didi said, her wary gaze taking in our battle-worn appearance.

Gavin paled a little at the sight of Samuel's injury.

Detective Johnson frowned. "I take it Ludvik escaped?"

"Yes." I fisted my hands. "And he's far more dangerous than we'd realized."

Our earpieces crackled to life, startling us and causing Gavin's horns to pop out.

"The cameras are back online," Nigel said somberly.

Detective Johnson choked on a gurgle when a translucent figure materialized beside us.

It was Mindy. She flickered in and out of visibility, shaken and disheveled.

"I'm sorry. I tried to stop her!"

I stared. "Stop who?"

"The ghost." Mindy met our puzzled gazes, her eyes wide with fear. "That vampire is forcing a ghost to help him. A wraith. That's why the cameras have been going dark. This wraith—she's been dead a long time but she's bound to him, somehow." Her expression crumpled. "I could feel her pain. Whatever he's doing to her, it's hurting her badly."

"He must have an object of hers," Barney said

flintily. "Something her soul is chained to in the mortal realm."

Dread squeezed my heart as Didi and I did our best to comfort Mindy.

"I know it's a lot to ask, but do you think you can track her?" Samuel asked the ghost quietly.

Mindy sniffed and nodded reluctantly. "I'll try. It won't be easy."

"Just do your best," Samuel said.

I looked around. "Where's Bo?"

Our earpieces crackled to life before anyone could answer.

"I hate to be the bearer of bad news but we have another situation," Nigel said cagily.

We traded another round of fraught glances.

"What kind of situation?" Samuel asked warily.

"The kind that involves Abby's dog trying to arrest a vampire."

# DOMESTIC INVESTIGATIONS

"I'M TELLING YOU, THAT VAMPIRE WAS DEFINITELY UP TO something," Bo insisted from the back seat for the fifteenth time since we'd left the Hawthorne mansion. "He had shifty eyes."

He had his nose stuck to the Bentley's window again and was leaving marks on the glass that would probably involve some kind of detailing to get off, judging from the way Samuel's fingers kept twitching on the steering wheel every time he looked at my dog.

"All vampires have shifty eyes," Pearl said from her permanent perch on Victoria's lap. She swished her tail lazily. "It comes with the territory of being a predator."

"This was different," Bo protested. "He kept looking around like he was casing the joint."

"He was probably trying to figure out why a Husky was interrogating him about his grocery habits," Samuel said darkly.

"What exactly did Bo do?" Victoria asked. "Wait, never mind. I don't want to know."

I swallowed a sigh. The Hawthornes were getting the full Husky experience, whether they wanted it or not.

"I was being thorough," Bo huffed. "Real detectives ask follow-up questions."

"Real detectives don't corner random vampires and demand to know why they're loitering near blood banks," Samuel retorted.

"I'm telling you, he kept circling the block," Bo insisted. "Nobody needs to drive past a blood bank three times unless they're casing it."

Samuel's knuckles whitened on the steering wheel.

"Maybe he was lost," I intervened hastily.

"Vampires do have a bad sense of direction," Victoria observed.

Pearl's whiskers twitched. "I'm impressed the mutt can count to three."

"I can count much higher than that," Bo said proudly. "I know all the numbers up to—well, lots of them."

Samuel muttered something under his breath.

It was Sunday morning. We were on our way to Barney's place to discuss yesterday's incident at the blood bank and how to proceed from there. The vampire had been adamant the strategy meeting take place at his home and that the Tremaines be invited.

According to him, he and the vampire power couple had confidential information to share that could aid our investigation.

Didi, Gavin, and Detective Johnson had excused themselves from attending, probably because no amount of overtime pay could justify sharing the same breathing space as Victoria and the Tremaines.

It was Samuel who had advised bringing Pearl along for her historical perspective. I would have laughed had I not recalled the cat's various uncanny abilities, not to mention her talent for knowing things she had no business knowing. If we were about to dive into dark vampire secrets, having a supernatural feline with questionable origins and an attitude problem might actually be useful.

Victoria, on the other hand, had connections throughout Amberford's supernatural community and knew how to navigate vampire politics without accidentally starting a war. Plus, someone needed to keep Pearl from insulting anyone important enough to hold grudges.

Samuel turned onto a tree-lined street in Amberford's historic district, a few miles from the Hawthorne estate. I inspected the row of large Victorian houses sitting behind immaculate gardens and lawns so perfectly manicured they looked like someone had used a ruler to trim each blade of grass.

We were definitely in vampire territory.

Samuel pulled up in front of a three-story mansion painted in tasteful burgundy and cream. It sprawled across a large plot and had wings and annexes that seemed to have been added over the years.

"Barnabas has excellent taste," Victoria observed with approval.

I studied the eldritch weather vanes cautiously. "It's very, er, vampire-y."

Pearl sniffed. "They may serve tea in actual china cups here."

Bo's eyes gleamed with a morbid light. "I bet it'd be easy to bury bodies in the garden."

A familiar Rolls-Royce was already parked in the driveway.

"The Tremaines beat us here," Victoria noted.

I eyed the silver Audi behind Gregory's car with a puzzled frown. "Who else got invited?"

An uncomfortable expression danced across Samuel's face. "Virgil and Ellie."

I stiffened. "What? Why?!"

"Barney insisted," Samuel said. "He claimed this concerns them too."

My stomach did an uncomfortable flip, both at his words and the fact that he'd kept this a secret from me. I wasn't happy about my best friend potentially walking into danger. Again. The whole vampire-transformation thing was still too fresh in my mind.

What if she got hurt, or worse?

"Could you perhaps save the panic for an actual crisis?" Pearl said sharply. "Your anxiety is making the car smell like stress sweat."

"Fur Ball's right," Bo panted.

We climbed out of the Bentley before I could come up with a suitable riposte.

Barney's home was even more impressive up close. The shingle roof was adorned with gables sporting ornate Victorian woodwork and Gothic finials. Quaint bay and oriel windows protruded from the brick-and-decorative-wood-trimmed facade in unexpected places, adding to the mansion's rambling charm. Everything was perfectly maintained, from the brass door knocker shaped like a bat to the spotless stained glass and the topiary bushes framing the front lawn.

The place made my apartment look like a college dorm.

"I should have worn my bow tie," Bo remarked as we headed up a cobblestone pathway to a wraparound porch with intricate spindle work and whimsical newel posts.

"I shall buy you another one, for casual occasions," Pearl said graciously.

I was about to ask "With what money?" when we reached the wooden front door complete with Gothic motifs and oversized hinges.

Someone had put googly eyes on the bat brass knocker.

We stared.

The door opened before any of us could comment on this blatant anomaly. Barney appeared in a pair of perfectly pressed slacks, a crisp white shirt, and armed with his usual aloof expression. He froze at the sight of the googly eyes.

The vampire muttered something under his breath, peeled them off, and stuck the offending items in his pocket.

"Victoria, Samuel, Abigail." He nodded politely, the look he gave us indicating we were never to speak of what just happened. The vampire lowered his gaze to Bo and Pearl. "I see you brought the usual suspects."

"Hello, Barnabas," Victoria said pleasantly. "Thank you for hosting us."

Bo wagged his tail. "I smell cookies."

"My housekeeper just baked a fresh batch," Barney admitted. "Please, come in." He stepped aside.

The interior of the vampire's home was not what I thought it would be. The dark wood, expensive rugs, and furniture that was probably older than my grandparents I kinda expected. What I didn't anticipate was how lived-in it would feel.

"Nice place," I said, meaning it.

"Thank you. I've been here for a hundred and fifty years."

Bo gulped. "That's like, really old in dog years."

A vampire in a butler's uniform appeared from what I presumed was the direction of the kitchen. He was plump, pale, and carrying a silver tray laden with tea service.

"Ah." He smiled affably at our sight. "I see the rest of your guests have arrived, Master."

Barney made the introductions. "This is Harold, my butler."

An unholy cry rent the air somewhere at the back of the house before we could greet the butler. I let out a gargled sound. Pearl hissed and arched her back. Bo yelped and jumped behind me. Samuel and Victoria flinched.

Bar pursing their mouths, Barney and Harold looked otherwise unfazed.

A head popped out of a room down an impressive hallway to the left.

It was Ellie.

"What the heck was that?!" Her face brightened at the sight of me. "Hey, Abby!" She bounced down the corridor and engulfed me in a bear hug that almost broke my ribs.

"Oh. I'm sorry." My best friend grimaced at my wheeze. "Virgil warned me about the superstrength thing, but I'm still getting used to it. Hi, Victoria."

"Ellie," Victoria greeted cautiously while I tried to get my breath back. "You look very…healthy."

Ellie beamed. "I fed before I came."

Yup, I was never going to get used to hearing those kinds of words out of my best friend's mouth.

Virgil strolled behind Ellie, his expression wary. "What was that scream just now?"

"I apologize," Barney said, contrite. "That was Melvina, my housekeeper."

"She gets a tad melodramatic at times," Harold said apologetically.

On cue, heavy footsteps came from the direction where the butler had originally appeared. A dwarf with a braided beard and an unhappy expression traipsed into view, a baking tray in her mitt-covered hands. She had a battleaxe strapped to her back and was wearing an apron adorned with comical vampire-themed scenes.

Bo snickered at one of a vampire overreacting to garlic and another getting startled by sunlight.

I was pretty certain I was looking at the perp behind the googly eyes.

"It's a disaster, Master," the suspect blubbered. "The

latest batch of cookies—they—they came out wrong too!"

Our gazes dropped to the divine-smelling chocolate chip cookies she was presenting like some kind of natural disaster. They were shaped like bats.

Headless bats.

Ellie wiped some drool from the corner of her mouth. "Those look yum."

My best friend's newfound appetite for blood had evidently not impacted her sweet tooth.

"These things happen," Barney said patiently. "I'm sure they'll taste just fine." He narrowed his eyes slightly. "Incidentally, I confiscated another pair of googly eyes just now."

Melvina averted her gaze guiltily.

"They were to cheer you up, Master." She drew an abstract pattern on the floor with the toe of her steel-capped boot. "You've been kinda glum lately."

"I'm always glum," Barney said curtly. "It's my default expression."

I masked a grimace. At least the vampire had insight.

"How about you put those on a plate and bring them to the drawing room?" Harold told Melvina gently. "And lose the axe." The butler's tone got fractionally sharper.

"But it's a family heirloom," the dwarf protested. Her beard trembled at her employer's and the butler's stern looks. She twisted on her heels and stormed back toward the kitchen.

# 24

# CONFIDENTIAL AFFAIRS

BARNEY HEAVED A HEAVY SIGH LIKE THIS WAS A DAILY occurrence. He and the butler led the way down a hallway lined with oil paintings that were probably worth more than my car.

The informal sitting room they guided us to was spacious and comfortable, with overstuffed armchairs arranged around a marble fireplace and bay windows overlooking the gardens at the back. There were books scattered on a side table, a coffee mug on the mantelpiece, and what looked like a crossword puzzle abandoned on an antique escritoire.

Gregory and Constantia sat on a navy velvet sofa, the vampire couple looking a little tense in the relaxed surroundings.

Gregory rose and nodded stiffly in our direction when we entered. "Samuel. Victoria." His gaze lingered on me. "I heard you got injured fighting Ludvik?"

"It was Samuel who got hurt."

Surprise flared on Gregory's and Constantia's faces.

"It was just a scratch," my alpha said.

His wound had already healed, something I'd taken great pains to check last night.

We settled in the armchairs, Ellie and Virgil staying close to each other. I studied them with mixed feelings.

Three weeks ago, my best friend's biggest concern was whether the cute guy at the bar we regularly frequented had noticed her new haircut. Now she was dating a vampire and had become a brand-new member of the supernatural community I had longed to keep her away from.

Pearl gazed on approvingly as Harold served us tea in real china cups. Melvina brought in a serving tray piled with an assortment of supernatural-creature-shaped cookies in various states of dismemberment. The butler and the housekeeper retreated quietly to the door, a suspiciously axe-shaped outline stretching the back of the dwarf's dress.

Samuel waited until we'd helped ourselves to refreshments before addressing Barney. "So what was it you wanted to talk about?"

The vampire exchanged a guarded look with the Tremaines.

"Ancient vampire history and ideology."

"That sounds boring," Bo declared at my feet around the cookie he was busy scarfing down.

"But important under the circumstances, so why don't you can it, Mutt?" Pearl said coolly.

"I take it there's a point to all this?" I said warily while Bo sulked.

"Yes," Gregory confessed with an awkward

expression. "This situation with Ludvik—it's more complicated than we initially thought."

"We think we know what he's planning," Barney said. "And if we're right, my nephew is about to commit an abomination."

Bo gulped noisily. Pearl narrowed her eyes.

My pulse quickened. Barney and the Tremaines looked nervous. More nervous than I'd ever seen them before. And that in itself was scary.

"How so?" Samuel finally said stiffly, his tension humming across the mate bond.

"What we're about to reveal violates several centuries of vampire secrecy laws," Barney replied grimly. "Under normal circumstances, sharing this information with non-vampires would be considered treason."

"But these aren't normal circumstances," Gregory added.

Constantia nodded hesitantly.

"No," Barney agreed. "They're not." He took a deep breath. "The pureblood ideology Ludvik is a fan of isn't just about vampire supremacy. It's about fundamentally transforming what it means to be a vampire."

I felt the familiar prickle of unease that preceded really bad news.

"Is this about the ancient ritual you mentioned? The one that would allow Ludvik to absorb the powers of other bloodlines to make himself into a new breed of vampire?"

Barney nodded, his face tight.

"This ritual requires a blood sacrifice," Constantia said in a brittle voice.

There was a drawing of breaths across the room. Bo crawled quietly under my chair, his ears flat.

My heart thumped painfully against my chest. "You mean, he plans to kill someone?!"

Samuel clenched his jaw. Victoria frowned.

Barney and the Tremaines's silence was all the answer we needed.

Well, that explained why the vampires looked like they were at a funeral.

"This is a surprise," Pearl said sharply. "The ritual your nephew intends to use to make himself into a Vampire Lord is the Crimson Ascension?"

We all gaped at her, the vampires doubly shocked.

"The Crimson what now?" I mumbled.

"The Crimson Ascension," Pearl repeated dismissively, like I'd asked her the time of day. "It's the name of a forbidden ritual from the darkest chapters of vampire history."

Barney lowered his brows. "How do you know about that ceremony?"

"He's right." Gregory frowned heavily. "That ritual has been classified for centuries."

"I've been around long enough to learn some of your secrets," Pearl said evasively.

This appeared to impress Bo but bring little comfort to Barney and Gregory.

There was no end to Pearl's secrets it seemed.

I managed to set down my teacup with only a slight

tremor in my hands. "I'm going to need you people to start from the beginning."

A muscle jumped in Barney's cheek.

"Over a thousand years ago, a group of vampires sought the help of the fae and witches to create a gruesome rite," he began bitterly. "It required four key components: the sacrifice of a pureblood vampire from a powerful bloodline, the binding of a wraith to channel and amplify the transferred essence, a full moon to maximize the flow of supernatural energy, and a ley line to lock it all down."

Victoria gasped and covered her mouth with a hand.

My stomach lurched. I now understood the Alliance members' reactions, especially Melody's and Cornelius's.

"The wraith Mindy mentioned yesterday." I met Samuel's stunned gaze. "It must be why Ludvik needs her at his side!"

He nodded grimly.

"The ritual transforms a vampire into something beyond traditional vampire classification—a hybrid creature with enhanced speed, strength, and abilities that transcend the normal limitations of our race," Barney continued.

"It was banned by the vampire councils, and for good reason," Gregory added in a hard voice. "The new breed of vampire it produced was too unstable and unpredictable, posing a threat not only to the established order of the vampire councils, but to the wider supernatural community."

"Wait," Ellie quavered in a small voice, Virgil looking really nervous beside her. "Someone actually succeeded in performing this ritual?!"

A chilling silence followed. Gregory and Constantia shot uneasy looks at Barney.

Realization dawned. I stared at Barney, my mouth dry.

Samuel and Victoria looked equally dumbfounded. Only Pearl looked unsurprised.

"My grandfather was the first vampire to acquire that despicable power," Barney confirmed darkly.

A loud clunk made us all jump and Bo yelp.

Melvina had dropped the axe in her shock. The dwarf recovered the weapon sheepishly under Barney's frown.

The vampire sighed and rubbed the back of his neck tiredly. "The transformation my grandfather underwent was irreversible. It drove him to madness and eventually led to his execution by the vampire councils. His associates were all similarly terminated, as were the fae and witches who assisted them."

"Trying to contain multiple conflicting bloodline memories and powers would make anyone lose their mind," Pearl observed steadily.

Barney's expression darkened. "The way Ludvik fought yesterday tells me he may already have attempted the ritual. It's the only thing that can explain his erratic behavior and the unnatural abilities he demonstrated."

Bo poked his head out from under my chair.

"You mean the deranged humming?" he panted.

"I meant his speed and the way he was using the shadows to attack us."

I frowned as I recalled the dark trails Ludvik's presence had left in the air yesterday.

Pearl blinked lazily. "Capturing a wraith could certainly have given him that ability. A specter acts as a conduit to the other side and can bind otherworldly powers to a vampire's essence."

I clamped down on the urge to be sick.

Ellie asked the question at the top of everyone's mind. "How do we stop him?"

Barney traded another guarded look with the Tremaines.

"We find the object he stole from the wraith. And we use one of the most fundamental weaknesses a vampire has in order to defeat him."

Bo perked up. "You mean garlic?"

Barney blinked, nonplussed.

"No," he said, a hint of menace creeping into his voice.

"Holy water?" Bo hazarded with growing enthusiasm, oblivious to his growing peril. "A tanning bed?" He jumped to his feet and wagged his tail excitedly. "I know! Ellie's coffee."

"Hey!" my best friend protested.

"Her coffee's not that bad," Virgil said weakly.

I clocked Barney's death glare and hushed everyone.

The vampire waited until he had our undivided attention before speaking grimly.

"We stake him."

# 25

# STAKING 101

"I CAN'T BELIEVE THERE'S AN ENTIRE TRAINING FACILITY under our building," I muttered as I descended the stairs to the basement of Hawthorne & Associates the next morning. "Why wasn't I made aware of this?"

"It's on a need-to-know basis," Samuel replied cagily. "And until recently, you didn't need to know."

"Besides, you've been busy working out in other ways," Didi remarked tartly, her heels clicking on the concrete steps.

My face grew hot. Samuel's ears reddened.

Detective Johnson smirked. "I hear you two are at it like wild ani—"

Samuel stepped on the detective's foot.

"What they really mean is, they don't trust you not to accidentally wreck the place," Gavin said morosely while Detective Johnson cursed and hopped on his non-injured foot.

I shot the dragon newt a puzzled look as we

reached the bottom landing. "I've never wrecked anything."

Didi narrowed her eyes. "He meant himself. Someone got a little excited when he first learned about this place and tried to scan one of our clients in his distraction."

Bo carefully edged away from Gavin.

"He tried to scan a client?" I asked skeptically.

"It was a pixie." Samuel shuddered. "The copy machine broke. Mindy was livid."

"That ghost didn't stop wailing for a week," Didi said, still eyeing Gavin accusingly.

The dragon newt had the grace to look guilty.

"Your workplace is a nuthouse," Bo told me unhelpfully as we navigated a gloomy corridor.

"Ditto," Detective Johnson said.

A reinforced steel door with a digital security pad appeared at the end.

Bo brightened when Samuel typed in a code. "This is very spy-movie-like. I bet this place looks like one of those secret lairs the good guys use."

"Don't get your hopes up," Samuel muttered.

The secret lair my Husky had been expecting turned out to be more like a high-end gym than a superhero training facility. It had padded walls, rubber flooring, and the kind of reinforced equipment that suggested the place saw some serious supernatural action.

"Wow." Bo visibly deflated. "This place is a dump."

He padded over to investigate a collection of chew

toys that were clearly designed for creatures with much larger jaws than his.

"Those are for stress management," Didi explained at my wary expression. "Janet comes down here for her howling sessions."

"Every Friday at exactly three-thirty," Gavin said promptly. "Sometimes on Mondays too, depending on how the weekend went and whether she crossed paths with a certain witch."

Didi sniffed haughtily.

I grimaced. I knew Janet stress-howled. I hadn't realized she did it at work.

I was still processing this revelation when Barney appeared from an equipment room. The vampire looked like the world's most reluctant gym teacher as he carried an armload of wooden stakes and a few hammers, and lugged an actual coffin complete with brass handles and a heavy wooden lid behind him.

Bo's ears flattened at the sight of the coffin.

"Right, then," Barney said grimly, setting the coffin on the floor and the stakes on a nearby table. "Before we begin, there's something I need to remind everyone of." His expression grew even more serious, which I hadn't thought was possible. "The next full moon is tomorrow night."

I could have told him that. My skin and bones were itching like crazy and I could feel all the other telltale signs that told me my wolf was dying to cut loose.

"Which means Ludvik's timeline just became much more urgent," Barney continued. "If he's planning to complete the ritual, he'll need the full moon's power to accomplish his goal."

Didi exchanged an uneasy glance with Gavin and Detective Johnson. Barney had sworn them to secrecy that morning before telling them about the secret ritual.

"So we have less than two days to stop him," Samuel said tightly.

"Less than that, actually," Barney said. "The ritual would need to begin at moonrise on the night of the full moon. Which gives us roughly thirty hours to locate him and end this."

No pressure, then.

Barney gestured to the stakes. "This is why you all need to learn how to stake a vampire properly."

Didi raised her hand. "Question. When you say 'stake a vampire,' are we talking about the traditional wooden-stake-through-the-heart method?"

Barney curled a lip. "That's a myth perpetuated by humans who clearly never tried to penetrate vampire skin with a piece of wood."

Bo tilted his head, his eyes taking on a familiar morbid gleam. "So how do you actually stake a vampire?"

"You nail their coffin shut while they're inside it."

We stared.

"Come again?" Detective Johnson asked carefully.

"A vampire can only be truly staked while they're in their resting place," Barney explained. "The coffin acts as a containment vessel. You drive iron nails through the lid, pinning them inside, and then stake the coffin itself to consecrated ground."

I scratched my cheek. "That seems unnecessarily complicated. Also, do we even have consecrated ground around these parts?"

Barney frowned. "It's supposed to be complicated. We're not exactly designed to be easy to kill. And it's easy to make consecrated ground."

Bo wagged his tail excitedly. "Let me guess. A dash of holy water, right?!"

"No," Barney said irritably. "All it takes is the blood of a virgin and a prayer."

Didi and I exchanged a cautious glance in the hush that followed.

"The virgin part could prove to be a problem," I volunteered with a grimace. "And I'm pretty sure the rest of Amberford is running low on that item too."

"It doesn't have to be a woman," Barney said.

We all turned to Gavin.

The dragon newt's horns popped out.

"Why are you all looking at me?!" he protested.

"You seem the most likely candidate in the room to fit the condition," Detective Johnson said with brutal honesty.

"Well, I'll have you know I'm not, okay?!" Steam puffed out of Gavin's nostrils.

"It can be any species," Barney grunted.

Bo huffed indignantly when he became the focus of our wary stares. "I've had some lady friends!"

I narrowed my eyes. "Oh yeah? Who?"

The Husky carefully avoided my gaze.

Samuel sighed heavily and indicated the wooden stakes on the table. "So these are for practice?"

"Yes," Barney said. "The key is not to aim for the heart. That won't kill us, but it will make us extremely angry. Instead, you want to target the joints."

"The joints?" I echoed.

"Shoulders, hips, knees," Barney demonstrated on himself. "A properly placed stake will pin the limb and prevent movement. It's painful and debilitating, but not fatal."

"That's horrible," Gavin said, looking queasy.

"Better horrible than having your veins sucked dry," Barney snapped. "And given that Ludvik has absorbed a wraith's abilities, traditional vampire combat techniques won't work on him. This may not be much help, but it might be your only option to slow him down."

Didi picked up one of the stakes and examined it critically. "They look like they've been modified."

"Iron cores wrapped in wood," Barney confirmed. "The iron prevents vampire healing, the wood provides grip. The iron also reduces the chance of the stake shattering on impact."

"Smart," Detective Johnson said approvingly.

"I have my moments," Barney said coolly. "Now, help me bring out the dummies."

Five minutes later, we were facing a collection of training dummies arranged along the far wall. They were humanoid in shape and clearly built to withstand supernatural abuse judging by the scorch marks and claw gouges decorating their surfaces.

Someone had put googly eyes on their faces.

"Melvina needed cheering up," Barney said defensively at our leaden stares.

"Right," I murmured. "About the coffin."

"It's for demonstration purposes."

"That's both reassuring and deeply weird," Detective Johnson observed while I swallowed a sigh of relief.

Barney sniffed. "Let's begin with basic stance and grip."

The vampire went on to demonstrate proper staking technique on the practice coffin. The gravity of the situation was slightly ruined by Didi asking questions and taking notes, while Bo added a running commentary that featured lines like "Shouldn't you yell something when you do that?" and "In your face, bloodsucker!" None of this was helped by Gavin's tendency to accidentally singe things when he got excited.

"How about we move on to the dummies?" Samuel suggested hastily when Barney's eyes began glowing crimson.

"I think that's a great idea," the vampire ground out.

I was soon lining up for my first practice throw.

"Remember," Barney instructed. "You're not trying to pin a butterfly to a board. You need force and precision."

I hefted the stake, aimed for the dummy's shoulder joint, and let it fly.

It bounced off the dummy's chest and clattered to the floor.

Bo sat down and scratched his ear. "Well, that was embarrassing."

I narrowed my eyes at the Husky. "That's gold coming from someone without opposable thumbs."

Samuel stepped up behind me while Bo huffed indignantly. "Here, let me show you."

His hands covered mine, adjusting my grip and stance. The familiar warmth of the mate bond flared between us, making it suddenly very difficult to concentrate on vampire-staking techniques. I bit my lip.

"Focus on the target," he murmured in my ear, his breath sending shivers down my spine while his heat and scent flooded my senses. "Don't overthink it."

My wolf stood to attention. I tried to focus on the dummy instead of the way Samuel's body felt pressed against mine. It was harder than it should have been, especially considering we were less than two days away from the full moon.

"Now," he said softly.

It took all my willpower to ignore the way my wolf was panting lecherously and release the stake. This time it hit the dummy square in the shoulder joint with a satisfying thunk.

"Much better," Barney said approvingly. "Although we could all have done without the romantic coaching."

"Yeah, how about we focus on not dying?" Didi said pointedly.

Heat flooded my cheeks as Samuel stepped back with a slight smile.

Damn my alpha and his sexy moves.

Detective Johnson was up next. His first throw hit the dummy's center mass with enough force to embed the stake six inches deep.

Gavin sniffed. "Show off." The dragon newt promptly set his stake on fire before he could throw it.

Didi cursed and grabbed a fire extinguisher from the wall.

By the time we de-sparked Gavin and moved on to close-combat techniques, I was starting to feel like we might actually have a chance against Ludvik. The key, according to Barney, was working as a team and not trying to be dumb heroes.

"Vampires are designed to hunt alone," he explained as he demonstrated a defensive position. "We're not used to coordinated attacks from multiple opponents. Use that against him."

"We tried that yesterday," I reminded him.

"This time, we'll know what to expect."

Samuel frowned. "What about his speed?"

"Anticipation." Barney sighed at our expressions. "He's fast, but he's also predictable. Vampires, even enhanced ones, have patterns. Study his movements, predict where he'll be, not where he is."

"That sounds easier said than done," I muttered.

"Everything worthwhile is," Barney replied.

Detective Johnson looked like he'd been mulling something over for a while. He finally spoke.

"What if we can't find his coffin?"

His words were followed by a fraught silence.

Barney lowered his brows. "Then we'll have to find another way to stop him."

"Like what?" I asked warily.

Barney hesitated. "I honestly don't know."

Before anyone could respond to this less-than-encouraging statement, footsteps pounded down the basement stairs. Nigel appeared, a few tentacles writhing in agitation around his head and his face flushed from running.

"You need to come," he gasped. "Now!"

"What's wrong?" Samuel asked sharply.

My chest tightened. "Has there been another attack?!"

Nigel shook his head. "No! It's Mindy. She thinks she's found something." The boogeyman shone brightly, causing us to squint. "And you're never going to believe where!"

# 26

# UNDER THEIR NOSES

I frowned at the building in front of us.

Though it was daytime, the Chamber of Commerce still looked the same as it had the last two occasions I'd been there—imposing, official, and soul-crushingly boring. Which, I realized grimly as we approached the main entrance, was probably part of its appeal as a hiding spot.

"*This* is where he was hiding all along?" Didi asked skeptically.

Mindy had been trying to track down the wraith all weekend. No one had been more surprised than Barney at the location where she'd identified a trace of its passage that morning.

The ghost had already confirmed Ludvik was currently not on site.

Samuel frowned. "It kinda makes sense. The building's warded against unauthorized supernatural intrusion, but—"

"If you know the ward patterns, you can get in fairly easily," Barney said darkly.

"Plus, there's all that human and supernatural traffic," Detective Johnson observed thoughtfully.

Gavin nodded, horns popping out slightly. "There'd be different supernatural scents every day. They'd make for a perfect cover."

Bo's tail wagged. "It's like hiding in plain sight."

"How long does Mindy think he was down there for?" I asked uneasily.

"At least two weeks," Nigel replied. "Possibly longer."

I lowered my brows. Two weeks of Alliance meetings while Ludvik sat in the basement, probably listening to every word. In fact, he was probably in the building the first time I came here.

Barney clenched his jaw. "He's been playing us from the start."

A different security guard from the usual guy emerged from the building as we reached the doors. He had a clipboard in his hands and a busy expression. He frowned at the sight of us.

"Building's closed for maintenance," he called out. "Come back tomorrow."

Detective Johnson flashed his badge. "We're here on police business."

The guard squinted at it, then at our group. His gaze lingered on Gavin's smoking horns, Barney's stony face, and Bo's overenthusiastic expression.

"Yeah, I'm gonna need to see some paperwork," he said slowly. "Official authorization and all that."

Samuel narrowed his eyes. "We don't have time for paperwork. And you know damn well who I am."

The guard straightened to his full height. "Rules are rules, Mr. Hawthorne. I can't make exceptions for—" He stopped abruptly, his eyes rounding. A choked gurgle left him. He dropped his clipboard and backed away several steps.

We looked around. Detective Johnson paled.

Half a dozen tentacles writhed semi-menacingly around Nigel's head. His face had sprouted five extra pairs of eyes.

"We really need to get in there," the boogeyman said, chin jutting forward. "The fate of this town rests on it."

The guard fumbled for his keys, his back pressed so hard against the wall he looked like he was about to climb it.

"Yeah, okay, whatever you need!"

He dropped the keys in his panic and squealed.

Samuel picked them up. "Thank you. Your cooperation is much appreciated."

"You were like a superhero," Bo told Nigel in an awed voice as we filed past the pale, sweating, and now hyperventilating guard.

"It's nothing special," Nigel said shyly.

"How about you lose the tentacles and extra eyes before I lose my breakfast?" Detective Johnson said weakly.

"Oh. Right. Sorry."

Mindy materialized beside us when we were

halfway across the foyer, her translucent form flickering with excitement.

"Great, you're here. I've been analyzing the residual ectoplasmic frequencies in the building and cross-referencing them with the ambient supernatural energy readings from around Amberford. If I factor in the temporal decay rates of wraith essence—"

Didi grimaced and put a hand up. "English, please."

Mindy sagged a little.

"I tracked the wraith," she admitted semi-sullenly.

"You could have led with that," Detective Johnson said skeptically.

"It's more complicated than normal tracking," Mindy protested. "The wraith's energy signature was creating a hybrid resonance pattern that—"

"How about we save the science lesson for another day?" Samuel interrupted with a heavy sigh.

Mindy's eyes flashed brightly, a sure-fire sign she was getting irritated.

"She's not going to start doing spooky stuff, is she?" Detective Johnson whispered to Didi. "Poltergeist activity freaks me out."

"Not if she knows what's good for her," Didi muttered, eyeing Barney's darkening expression. She squinted at the detective. "And how come a werewolf is afraid of ghosts?"

"Childhood trauma. I don't want to talk about it."

Barney looked like he was considering exorcising people.

"Where to?" I asked Mindy hastily.

"One of the subbasements. You guys need to take the elevator."

The service corridors Mindy led us down were dimly lit and smelled like industrial cleaning supplies and old coffee. The building was eerily quiet. Our footsteps echoed as we navigated the passageways, the sound bouncing off the concrete walls.

"It's a good thing we're not aiming for the element of surprise," Didi murmured.

"When do you think they were last here?" Samuel asked Mindy as the elevator came into view.

"My best guess? Six to eight hours ago. I tried to follow the wraith's trail from here but it goes cold outside the building." The ghost hesitated and shot an uneasy look at us over her shoulder where she floated ahead. "It looks like they left in a hurry."

The elevator ride to the subbasement was tense and silent. The doors finally opened with a grating squeak.

We were hit with a wave of stale air that made my nose wrinkle. Underneath it was something else. Something that made my wolf's hackles rise.

"You smell that?" I asked Samuel cautiously.

He frowned. "Yes. But I can't quite place it."

Didi narrowed her eyes. "That's magic. *Old* magic."

"She's right," Barney confirmed sourly. "He's definitely been practicing his ritual down here."

The subbasement was a maze of storage rooms and utility corridors. The low lighting cast everything in harsh shadows as we navigated the passages, the air possessing the dead quality of places that never saw natural light.

"This way," Mindy said.

She hurried around a corner, Nigel following closely.

We found the ghost and the boogeyman in front of the door to what had once been a storage room.

It was currently hanging off its hinges.

Inside, boxes of documents were scattered across the floor, their contents spilled and trampled as if by someone in a fit of rage. Filing cabinets stood open, drawers pulled out and dented.

My stomach clenched at the sight of the dark stains splattered across the walls and ground. Bo pressed close to me, his tail down.

"Is that—?" I asked.

"Blood," Barney confirmed. He took a careful sniff of the air. "Fresh. Maybe six hours old, which matches Mindy's estimation of when they were last here."

"Human or vampire?" Detective Johnson asked, his tone suggesting he didn't really want to know.

Barney knelt beside one of the larger stains, touched it, and rubbed his fingers.

"Vampire," he said flatly.

I studied his troubled expression warily. "What is it?"

"I can smell an artifact."

That was not the kind of news I wanted to hear. I had a bad history with artifacts.

"I bet it's the magic device he's been using for his ritual," Didi said.

Bo had been cautiously sniffing around the edges of the room. He froze all of the sudden.

"I think there's something here."

My pulse quickened as we joined him.

"We could do with some light," Didi muttered.

Nigel obliged and brightened a little. The faint outline of a door appeared in the wall.

Bo sat down, tail sweeping the floor. "I was right."

"Can you go through and see what's on the other side?" Samuel asked Mindy tensely.

She nodded and headed for the wall, only to bounce right off it.

"Mindy!" Tentacles shot out of Nigel's body as he tried to catch the ghost.

"I'm okay." Mindy straightened and shook herself, looking confused.

"What the heck was that?" Detective Johnson asked uneasily.

Mindy approached the wall and traced spectral fingers across it.

"There's a barrier. I think he had the wraith put it up." She frowned. "He must have known I would come looking."

I clenched my jaw. "Mindy, is this barrier metaphysical?"

She shot a startled look at me. "Yes. Why?"

"Good." I let my wolf slip under my skin, gathered our strength, and punched the wall.

It exploded inward. Bricks crumbled, outlining a large opening.

The smell of blood and magic that came from inside made Barney scowl and the rest of us gag. The vampire headed inside first.

The room was small and dark. Nigel gave us some more lighting. I looked around as the shadows retreated, revealing more blood on the floor and walls. Mindy watched us anxiously where she floated on the threshold, still unable to come through.

"Shit," Didi mumbled.

We followed her gaze to where Barney squatted in front of a makeshift altar at the far end. My chest tightened as we approached. A circle of strange symbols were carved into the floor. Dark candles sat in pools of their own wax around it.

The whole thing was giving me bad-juju vibes.

Samuel studied the setup with a hard expression. "Looks like he got pretty far into his preparations."

"But he didn't complete it, right?" I said, unable to mask the hope underscoring the question.

"No." Barney rose, his face locked in a thunderous expression. "He's still missing a key ingredient. A pureblood vampire."

"Hey, guys," Detective Johnson called out from a corner of the room. "You should see this."

We headed over to where he'd dropped on his haunches.

Papers were scattered across the floor. But these weren't old Alliance archives. They were documents with familiar logos and names on the letterheads.

"These are the medical records he stole from the blood banks he targeted." Samuel's voice was tight with anger.

"There's more," Detective Johnson said grimly.

He was holding a detailed map of Amberford. Red X's marked various locations throughout the city.

Didi scowled. "Blood banks, the hospital, the homes of vampires."

I fisted my hands. "He's been planning this for weeks."

"Months, more likely," Barney corrected. His eyes gleamed crimson as he looked around the secret room. "This setup took time to prepare. He didn't just decide to hide here on a whim."

I swallowed heavily at his meaning. This wasn't just a hiding place. It had been Ludvik's base of operations, where he'd studied his targets, made meticulous plans, and waited for the right moment to strike.

The more I got to know about this vampire, the more I felt like ripping his throat out.

"We have to tell the Alliance." I met Samuel's and Barney's gazes, my heart thundering against my ribs. "We're going to need extra help if we want to track him down before the full moon. Besides, they need to know Ludvik's been in the building all this time."

Samuel pinched the bridge of his nose. "Something tells me they're not going to take the news well."

I noticed Bo nosing at a stack of paper. "What is it?"

"I smell something," he huffed excitedly. His ears suddenly flattened. He whined and backpedaled behind me, his tail down.

I leaned down and picked up what he'd unearthed.

It was a blank piece of paper. My belly twisted when I turned it over.

Someone had scrawled "burn the doll" in blood on the other side.

# ACCUSATIONS AND VANISHING ACTS

THE EMERGENCY ALLIANCE MEETING THAT EVENING HAD all the warmth of a tribunal. The *Twilight Conference Room* buzzed with tension as supernatural leaders filed in, faces grim and tempers already frayed.

I sat between Samuel and Victoria, my stomach churning. Pearl observed the proceedings lazily where she perched on the armrest of Victoria's chair. Bo was unusually quiet next to me, the gravity of the situation evidently not lost on him. Barney maintained a stony silence beside the Tremaines, his expression still dark.

"This is a complete disaster," Titania muttered, her gossamer wings flickering with agitation.

"Disaster doesn't begin to cover it." Cornelius's fae features managed to look beautifully ethereal and depressingly glum at the same time.

Victoria shifted uneasily in her chair. I understood her discomfort. The room felt like it was one wrong word away from exploding.

Daria called the meeting to order with a sharp rap of her gavel.

"As you all know," she began, her voice cutting through the tension like a well-honed axe, "our security has been compromised. Ludvik Bludworth has been operating from the subbasement of this very building for at least two weeks."

"Two weeks!" Wendall's nostrils sparked with rage. "How the hell does a homicidal vampire set up shop under our noses without anyone noticing?"

"Because someone wasn't doing their job." Melody's voice carried an edge that could cut glass as she looked pointedly to her left.

Sulfur wafted weakly around Oscar as he slumped deeper into his shadowy corner. The demon's usual pompous demeanor had deflated and he looked like he'd rather be anywhere else but here.

"Oscar," Daria said with the kind of calm that preceded executions. "You're in charge of building security and maintenance. Care to explain how this happened?"

Oscar's zone of darkness shrank a little. "Well, the thing is…" He trailed off and gulped audibly.

My wolf wrinkled her nose. I could smell his fear from where I sat.

"The thing is what, Oscar?" Gregory's eyes flashed crimson.

"I may have, er, sublet some of the unused basement space," the demon mumbled.

I narrowed my eyes while the room exploded.

"You sublet Alliance space?!" Finnic roared amidst the cursing and protests. He slammed his fist down hard enough to make everyone jump. "What kind of idiot—?!"

"It was perfectly legal!" Oscar objected, puffing up slightly. "Those basement levels have been empty for decades. I thought, why not generate some extra revenue?"

"Revenue for what?" Daria asked, though her icy tone suggested she already knew the answer to her question.

I had my suspicions too, based on my first Alliance meeting.

"To fund"—*mumble mumble*—"for the"—*mumble mumble*, the demon said indistinctly.

Wendall leaned forward menacingly. "Care to repeat that?"

"To fund the expansion of Amberford's demon community, alright?!" Oscar blurted out.

Daria and I adopted similarly disgusted moues.

The demon continued. "We're severely underrepresented and I thought—"

"You thought you'd rent out secure Alliance space for your pet project?" Portia interrupted, her banshee voice hitting a pitch that made everyone wince.

Melody was studying Oscar like he was a bug she wanted to squash. "Did you even vet the tenant?"

Judging by Oscar's increasingly uncomfortable aura, it was clear the answer was no.

"The arrangements were made through a lawyer," he said, like that excused his actions. "He was very professional and paid six months in advance, cash. He told me the client valued privacy."

"Privacy," Barney repeated in a deadly voice. "A mysterious cash client who values privacy sublet the basement and that didn't raise any red flags?"

"Look, business is business," Oscar said defensively.

A low growl left Samuel.

Pearl jumped on the table.

"I see expecting competence from a demon who decorates his office with velvet paintings was overly optimistic," she said with arctic disdain.

Oscar spluttered. "Now, see here—!"

"No, you see here," Gregory snarled, rising from his chair. "Your incompetence has put every supernatural being in this town at risk! Never mind the innocent humans we cohabit with."

"It's easy to point fingers now," Wendall shot back, sparks popping from his nostrils. "But where was this concern when we voted against increased surveillance six months ago?"

"That was completely different," Titania protested, her wings buzzing.

"Is it?" Cornelius narrowed his eyes. "We've been so concerned with privacy that we've ignored basic security."

"Don't spread the blame around," Melody said sharply. "This is on Oscar."

"Actually," Finnic said icily, "I think we're missing the point."

The dwarf seemed remarkably calm, considering the circumstances.

Daria frowned. "Which is?"

"We're arguing about blame instead of solutions." He brought out an impressive battleaxe out from under the table. "Seems we'd accomplish more if we just cut down the demon first."

Not so calm after all.

Cornelius and Wendall grabbed the dwarf chieftain's arms as he lunged for Oscar.

"That dwarf's lost it," Bo panted while Oscar hastily retreated inside his kingdom of gloom.

I felt my blood pressure rise and swallowed a groan.

"Killing Oscar is not the solution, Finnic," Daria told the dwarf firmly as Cornelius and Wendall wrestled him into his chair and took his axe away.

"I mean, it would improve our moods," Melody said sourly.

"This is not the time for jokes!" Gregory snapped.

Titania nodded jerkily. Irritation surged through me.

Samuel shot a warning look my way when he picked up on my emotions.

"Gregory's right," my alpha said grimly. "If we don't work together, Ludvik will pick us off one by one. We're the only ones standing in the way of his crazy plans."

That sobered everyone up.

Pearl swished her tail coolly. "You fools need to get your act together."

Daria's eyes shrank to slits. "What we need is to track down Ludvik and eliminate him."

"Easier said than done," Barney said. "He's had weeks to prepare."

"So what do you suggest?" Melody snapped. "Wait for him to come to us?"

A fraught hush ensued. I glanced at the clock on the wall and clenched my jaw. We were wasting precious time.

"We should set a trap," Cornelius said. "Use bait he won't be able to resist." His gaze flickered to the Tremaines. "It seems he was after the blood of another powerful vampire lineage, after all."

The room's temperature dropped.

"Absolutely not," Gregory said, his voice so quiet the hairs rose on my nape.

Constantia's expression had grown feral beside her husband.

"I agree with Gregory." A muscle jumped in Barney's jawline. "It's too dangerous."

"It's logical," Cornelius pressed. "It's why he attacked the coffee shop where your son works—"

The power that flooded the chamber made everyone wince and had Bo shooting under my chair. My wolf stilled where she watched the proceedings from behind my eyes.

The air churned violently around Barney where he'd risen to his feet, his gaze a violent scarlet and his hands curled into fists at his sides.

"I said no," he growled.

I ignored the way the sound grated across my nerves and addressed the room coldly. "I agree with

Barney and Gregory. We cannot risk someone's life just to stop Ludvik."

Victoria nodded. "Abby's right."

Wendall crossed his arms and scowled. "Then what do you suggest we do, wolf?"

I bit down on a sharp retort and took a steady breath. "What Daria said. We find him first."

"How?" the dragon newt asked irritably. "He could be anywhere."

"Mindy and Nigel are trying to find the wraith working with Ludvik," I explained through gritted teeth. "They've already covered a lot of ground. We should help them as best we can."

There was still the small matter of the strange message we'd found in the hidden room in the subbasement. Mindy's best guess was that the wraith had left it. What it meant, no one yet knew.

"He can't have gone far," Samuel said, frowning. "The ritual requires specific conditions, namely a ley line."

Titania groaned. "Amberford is full of ley lines, Samuel."

"It's better than sitting here doing nothing," Samuel retorted.

"We need to pool resources," Portia said firmly. "Each faction contributes to the search and covers one area of town."

"Who coordinates?" Melody asked suspiciously.

"I will," Daria replied.

"Vampires should lead," Gregory protested. "It's our problem."

"Like hell it is," Finnic growled. "This affects everyone."

"Dwarves do have the best tracking ability," Titania murmured.

"Fae and witches have underground connections," Melody countered.

Cornelius dipped his chin.

The thin thread of my sanity finally snapped. The power I'd manifested at Springhill General flooded my veins and lit up my blood. The chandelier trembled and the floor shook as I stood up, my nails and fangs lengthening even as I maintained my human form.

Gasps echoed around the room. The Alliance members pushed back hastily from the table, their stunned gazes locked on me as my wolf's powers buffeted them.

"What the—?!" Daria mumbled.

"Calm down, Abby," Victoria said tensely.

"Now is not the time for this," Pearl added sternly.

Cornelius recovered first and narrowed his eyes. "It seems you've been hiding the truth about your luna powers."

The other Alliance members exchanged wary glances.

"She wasn't hiding anything," Samuel snapped.

An unholy growl left my throat. I was about to speak when my wolf froze. My head snapped to the doors, my instincts screaming danger.

Something had just entered the building.

Something that was moving fast and seething with rage.

Barney and the Tremaines stood up, power rolling off them as they took a defensive stance. Amber lit up Samuel's eyes as he rose in a half crouch, ready to transform at a moment's notice.

"What the hell is that?!" Wendall hissed, horns flaming and tail out.

"I don't know, but I don't like it," Melody murmured tensely.

Magic bloomed around Daria's hands. Portia's hair unraveled. Bo hugged the floor under my chair.

"Oh." Pearl blinked and relaxed fractionally. "How interesting."

The doors of the conference room slammed open before any of us could make sense of her words.

Ellie burst in, hair disheveled and eyes glowing a red so vivid, her pupils looked like they were filled with blood. The air boiled around her, the power she wielded almost matching mine.

"He took him!" she snarled, her fangs gleaming. "That asshole took Virgil!"

I blinked, my rage fading to shock.

"What?" Gregory mumbled.

Constantia gripped her husband's arm tightly, her face ashen.

Ellie squeezed her eyes shut for a moment. "Virgil was supposed to meet me for dinner, but he never showed up," she ground out. "When I went to his apartment, the door was open and there were signs of a struggle." She swallowed convulsively. "I could smell him. I could smell the bastard who turned me!"

I moved and hugged Ellie, my heart pounding heavily.

My best friend froze before shuddering, her arms locking tightly around me.

Gregory's voice was barely controlled when he spoke. "We have to find them. *Now!*"

Constantia sat down heavily, a raw sound of pain leaving her.

Victoria and Titania rushed over to console her.

The rest of the Alliance members traded tense looks.

"All disagreements are tabled for now," Daria said in a hard voice. "We have less than twenty-hours until the full moon. That's our deadline."

# WAITING FOR WORD

THE CHAMBER OF COMMERCE FELT LIKE A MAUSOLEUM the next morning. Exhausted Alliance members and their teams had been trickling in since dawn, all bearing the same news. There was no sign of Ludvik, no trace of Virgil, and no leads worth following.

I sat on the second-floor landing, nursing my third cup of coffee and watching the steady stream of exhausted Alliance members reporting their failures. Gregory paced by the windows, his usual composure fraying at the edges. Constantia sat rigidly on the leather sofa beside Victoria, her hands clenched so tightly around the cup in her lap it was a miracle it hadn't shattered. Every few minutes, she would glance at her phone, hoping for news that never came.

Barney stood talking to Daria in a corner of the lobby, his expression darker than a thundercloud. He'd spent the night tracking down every vampire contact he had in three states, calling in favors and making threats with equal measure.

Unfortunately, it looked like he'd been right. Ludvik's new abilities meant he could mask his presence easily. Add to that the wraith he had entrapped and I couldn't help but feel we were fighting a losing battle.

"Anything?" Samuel appeared by my side, his hair still damp from a shower. He'd been out with Detective Johnson and the werewolf search teams all night and had used the bathing facilities in the building to freshen up.

"Nothing." The word tasted bitter in my mouth. "Where's Detective Johnson?"

"He went home to get some sleep." He pulled me up to my feet and kissed my forehead. "We'll find them."

I swallowed and nodded. We headed downstairs.

Ellie sat cross-legged on the floor next to Bo, absently scratching behind his ears while staring at nothing. She'd been like that for hours, her new vampire senses stretched to their limits as she tried to detect any trace of Virgil's scent. Though exhaustion showed in every line of her body, I could feel the coiled tension beneath it. She was ready to snap.

She looked up at our approach.

"He's out there somewhere," she told me wretchedly, her voice barely above a whisper. "I can feel it. And he's scared."

I sat down beside her. "Can you sense where?"

Ellie shook her head, frustration etched across her face. "It's too faint. Like an echo of an echo."

Bo whined and put a paw on her knee.

Samuel followed my gaze as I glanced at the large clock above the reception desk. He frowned.

We had less than twelve hours before the full moon rose.

"Where is Hugh?" I asked, partly to break the oppressive silence.

"He's checking out the forest north of Amberford with Caroline and Kent."

The sound of footsteps at the entrance made everyone tense, but it was only Titania arriving with a group of pixies I didn't recognize. She looked as exhausted as the rest of us.

"Nothing in the Crossroads," she reported to the lobby in general. "We checked every building, every basement, every abandoned lot. If he was there, he's gone now."

Gregory's jaw clenched. "What about the warehouse district?"

"Cornelius and his people covered that last night," Daria reported, coming over with Barney. "Also nothing."

"The docks?" Constantia asked hopefully.

Amberford sat on the confluence of two rivers and had an extensive dock area.

"Melody's teams searched there at dawn," Titania replied tiredly, settling into an empty chair. "Same result."

It felt like we were trapped in some kind of horrible loop. Question, negative answer, growing desperation, repeat.

Samuel's phone rang. The sound cut through the

room like a gunshot. Everyone's attention snapped to him. He answered the call and put his phone on speaker, a muscle jumping in his jawline.

"Didi, please tell me you and Gavin have something."

"We found him." Didi's voice was tight with exhaustion but carried a note of triumph that made my heart skip. "Mindy tracked the wraith's energy signature to an abandoned mine about twenty miles west of town. Nigel's with her."

Gregory was on his feet in an instant, Constantia right behind him. Barney's expression shifted from frustration to deadly focus in a heartbeat.

"Are you certain?" Gregory demanded harshly, storming over.

"As certain as we can be," Didi replied. "Mindy says the wraith's signature is stronger than at the Chamber of Commerce. She thinks the wraith has been there since yesterday."

I clenched my jaw. Ludvik had stayed one step ahead of us all this time. I hoped his luck was about to run out.

"What about Virgil?" Constantia quavered.

"We can't tell from here, but"—Didi hesitated—" there are definitely signs of recent vampire presence. Gavin found a dead deer. It was a fresh kill."

"Where exactly is this place?" Samuel asked tensely.

"It's in dwarf territory," Didi replied. "Old mining country. Finnic should know of it."

Surprise widened Daria's eyes. She disappeared and returned with a detailed topographical map.

"Here!" We gathered around her as she spread the map on a coffee table. She pointed at a location in the forest to the west of Amberford. "This must be the place."

I felt a spark of hope for the first time in hours. "Can we get inside without being detected?"

"That's the tricky part," Didi said awkwardly. "Mindy says the mine has multiple entrances, but most of them are collapsed or flooded. She and Nigel didn't venture too deeply inside." The witch paused. "Finnic might know a passage that's still passable."

"Where's Finnic?" Gregory asked in a strained voice.

Samuel frowned. "Still out searching."

"I'll call him," Titania said hastily.

"The mine's main entrance is hidden in a valley between two ridges," Didi continued. "There's an old access road, but it's overgrown."

"I know of it." Barney frowned. "That was a clever move by Ludvik."

"Why?" I asked warily.

"That whole area is full of traps." The vampire met my gaze. "Which means it's going to be dangerous for a large team to get in that mine."

"Traps?" I echoed weakly.

"Dwarves are very protective of their properties," Samuel said darkly.

"It doesn't matter," Ellie said tightly. "We're going."

I furrowed my brow. "Ellie—"

"No," she cut me off, her eyes blazing. "Don't even

think about trying to talk me out of this. I'm coming with you!"

Bo whined and pushed in between us.

Frustration churned my insides. I could tell there would be no changing Ellie's mind.

"I know what you're worried about Abby, but I can handle myself," my best friend said, her voice taking on an edge I'd never heard before. "In case you missed it last night, I'm not exactly helpless anymore."

My chest tightened. I couldn't deny the power Ellie had exhibited when she'd stormed the building. It had even given Barney and Pearl pause, after all.

"Alright," I said reluctantly.

Gregory and Constantia exchanged a look I couldn't quite read.

"I'm not putting my son's life at risk for anyone," Gregory stated, his eyes glinting with menace. "If you come, you follow orders. No heroics, no improvisation."

"Agreed," Ellie said immediately.

"And if things go wrong, you get out," I added in a hard voice. "No arguments, no looking back."

Ellie hesitated for just a moment and nodded curtly. "Alright."

"I still don't like it," Titania said uneasily. "A newly turned vampire is too unpredictable."

Daria sighed. "Neither do I, but we might need her abilities."

It was another half hour before Finnic arrived.

"I heard the news," the dwarf said grimly as he stormed inside the building. "That bastard really chose to hide in one of our abandoned mines?!" He slammed his axe blade down on the coffee table.

For once, no one protested.

"Yes," Samuel said curtly. "Didi says a lot of the entry points aren't passable. Do you know a way to get inside?"

"Don't worry your wolfy head about that," Finnic said dismissively. "Everyone gear up and meet back here. We leave within the hour. That should give me enough time to assemble my best warriors."

Bo followed me as I headed for the stairs. "I'm coming with you."

I stopped and frowned at the Husky. "A mine is really not the kind of place I should be taking a dog."

"But I'm no ordinary dog," Bo huffed.

"He's right." Pearl padded quietly toward us. "Take the mutt, wolf."

I frowned at the cat's sphinx-like expression. "Is there something you're not telling me?"

Pearl twitched her whiskers. "Paranoia really doesn't suit you. I just think he might come in handy."

"Fur Ball," Bo whined. He tried to lick the cat.

Pearl booped him on the nose. "Stop that. It's disgusting."

# UNDERGROUND WARRIORS

THE ENTRANCE TO THE ABANDONED MINE LOOKED LIKE A portal to Hell with a No Trespassing sign. Basically, exactly the kind of place where an evil vampire might take a hostage to complete an ancient ritual that would make him super evil.

Bo wagged his tail enthusiastically. "This place looks cool."

"This isn't a sightseeing tour," Samuel reminded my dog sternly.

"I know that," Bo protested. His voice dropped to a whisper. "But still. *Way* cool."

Gregory narrowed his eyes at the Husky.

I swallowed a groan, regret for bringing Bo already setting in. I had a feeling my dog's newfound enthusiasm for mines was going to become a terminal problem before this was over.

It had taken us an hour to make it here once we'd left our cars on the access road. Samuel had proposed the wolves transform and go ahead with the vampires, but Finnic had insisted we stay together.

"You seem be forgetting that this valley is littered with traps and sink holes," the dwarf chieftain had said grimly. "Dwarves know how to look out for them. The last thing me and my warriors need is to be picking pieces of werewolves and vampires off wooden spikes and cave floors."

I shot a wary glance at said warriors where we stood at the edge of the tree line. The first dwarf was Melvina, Barney's housekeeper. She was wearing chain mail over a different vampire-themed apron, had her battleaxe strapped to her back, and was examining a wooden stake with professional interest.

The second dwarf was Hilda from the hospital. Her medical supplies were integrated into her armor and she had a first aid kit that appeared to double as a weapon.

"Don't worry," she'd told us matter-of-factly when she'd caught us staring. "I've treated more combat injuries than most field medics. Occupational hazard of working the supernatural ward. Why, I once performed emergency surgery on a troll with nothing but a butter knife and some dental floss."

Mindy had flickered warily where she'd floated beside us.

"And I defeated three pixies in hand-to-hand combat just last week," Melvina had chimed in cheerfully. "They were trying to put glitter in Master Barney's coffee," she'd been at pains to explain.

"That was not hand-to-hand combat," Barney had

muttered. "You chased them around the kitchen with the flambé torch."

"Details, Master," Melvina had waved dismissively.

"They're my nieces," Finnic had said defensively at our skeptical looks. "And they're tougher than they look."

Somehow, Melvina and Hilda being related to Finnic had come as no surprise to anyone.

The rest of Finnic's team consisted of a grizzled dwarf who introduced himself as Leoric Ironfist, a fierce-looking female warrior called Belinda Stonebreaker, and a shifty-looking dwarf who went by Wildred Tunnelwalker. Wildred looked like he could navigate a maze blindfolded and empty your pockets while he was at it.

Didi watched the dwarf crew with an expression that said she was seriously reconsidering every decision that had led her here.

"This is going to be a disaster," Gavin muttered. He nervously adjusted the fire extinguisher collection strapped to his chest.

Samuel had insisted the dragon newt bring them along considering his natural tendency to incinerate anything that moved when he got nervous. No one wanted friendly fire in the confined space of a mine.

Ellie had been quiet since we'd arrived, her attention focused on the mine entrance. She raised her head abruptly, her eyes flashing red in the fading afternoon light.

"That bastard is definitely in there. I can smell him!

And"—her expression darkened—"I can smell blood and magic."

A feral sound left Gregory's throat. He leaned forward, like he was about to bolt for the entrance.

Barney took hold of his arm before he could move. "It isn't Virgil's."

My pulse spiked when Gregory hissed and whirled around, his face distorted in a monstrous mask that caused the dwarves to clutch their battleaxes and Gavin's nostrils to spark.

Barney didn't bat an eyelid. "Unless you want your son to die, I suggest you calm down."

Gregory took a shuddering breath. His features gradually settled down, along with my heart rate.

"We're wasting time," he ground out.

"We're not," Finnic said, frowning. "Look, I get why you want to rush in there, but the others are still getting into position."

The dwarf chieftain had directed Hugh, Nigel, Constantia, Detective Johnson and his team, and the rest of the Alliance to cover Ludvik's potential escape routes. There were more of them than Didi and Gavin had initially identified. Though Constantia hadn't been happy about being separated from her husband, she'd agreed to Finnic's plans.

As Daria had put it, this was the dwarf's rodeo.

My bones itched and my skin tightened as we waited for the signal. I glanced at the darkening sky where it was visible through the canopy. The full moon was only a few hours away and my wolf was dying to escape my human form.

My shoulders knotted when Finnic's walkie-talkie crackled into life.

Daria's voice came through. "We're in position."

"Roger that." The dwarf looked around. "Everyone ready?"

There was a low chorus of agreement.

Finnic lowered his brows. "Let's do this."

The main entrance gaped in the hillside as we approached the mine entrance in formation—Finnic and his dwarves in front, followed by Samuel, Gregory, and Barney, then me, Mindy, and Ellie. Didi and Gavin brought up the rear while Bo trotted alongside me, the Husky quiet for once.

The mine's entry point was larger than it had appeared from a distance. Old support beams framed the opening and rusted rails disappeared into the darkness beyond. The air that drifted out was cool and carried the scents Ellie and Barney had already identified—blood, magic, and something that made my wolf's hackles rise.

"This place is as cheerful as a tomb," Didi muttered.

"I used to mine here in the old days," Finnic grunted. "It has solid stone formations and great acoustics."

Bo perked up. "For singing?"

"For practicing our battle cries."

Bo deflated. "Oh."

I grimaced. For a rescue mission, this was turning out to be weirdly educational.

Gloom swallowed us as we moved deeper into the mine. Though our werewolf and vampire vision cut easily through the darkness, we turned on the flashlights the dwarves had provided us with. Made with secret dwarf technology, they were waterproof, shockproof, and guaranteed to work in the presence of hostile magic. They also worked well as a blunt weapon Hilda had confessed as she'd distributed them.

We soon reached a junction. Wind whistled faintly in the tunnel to our right. It brought with it a pungent smell that made Gavin gag and Didi wrinkle her nose.

"Bats," Finnic said, turning into the tunnel. "Watch your step. The floor will be slippery from guano."

"I hate bats," Mindy whispered.

"I hate mines," Gavin said glumly.

"I'm pretty much hating all of this," Didi declared grimly.

Our lights cast dancing shadows on the walls as we advanced, our footsteps echoing despite our best attempts at stealth. I could feel the weight of the mountain pressing down above us when we reached the next junction.

"How deep does this go?" Samuel asked in a low voice as we followed Finnic into the left branch.

"About four hundred feet at the deepest point," Finnic replied. "This mine was one of the largest of its time. It has multiple levels and lots of tunnels. It's a perfect place to hide."

"Or get lost," Didi muttered.

"That's what these are for," Melvina said, producing something from the pocket of her chain mail. "Trail markers."

Hilda and the other dwarves exchanged resigned looks. The rest of us stared.

"We are not marking our path with googly eyes," Barney said firmly.

"But they're practical, Master," Melvina protested. "Plus, these ones glow in the dark." She cocked her thumb over her shoulder, where she'd already stuck a pair to the wall.

Bo grinned and wagged his tail.

Gregory muttered something under his breath.

I was beginning to understand why Barney always looked exhausted.

After a short argument, Melvina was allowed to use her googly eyes to flag our route.

"We're gonna look stupid if we die in here and people find us by the glow of these things," Gavin muttered sullenly as we left a phosphorescent trail in our wake.

"We'll be dead, so we won't care," Didi pointed out.

"Death isn't that bad," Mindy protested.

Everyone chose to maintain a diplomatic silence at this.

We'd been walking for about ten minutes when Ellie suddenly stopped.

"They're close," she growled.

"She's right!" Mindy hissed. "I can smell the wraith!" Bo whined.

The rest of us couldn't smell much past the bat guano, but we were happy to take their word for it. A faint sound reached us as we cautiously crept forward.

We all froze and strained our ears.

At first, I couldn't hear anything but our breathing and the distant drip of water. Then I caught it.

It was music. Brooding, powerful music that was echoing from somewhere deep in the mine.

I shot a nervous glance at Barney. "Wait. Is that—?"

"Beethoven's Ninth Symphony," the vampire confirmed darkly.

Gregory rushed forward. "It's the ritual. It has to be!"

Finnic cursed as the vampire dropped his torch and disappeared into the gloom.

"Mindy, follow him!" Samuel barked.

We started running toward the music and whatever waited for us in the depths of the mine. Whatever it was, I just hoped we weren't too late.

# RITUAL INTERRUPTED

THE TUNNEL OPENED INTO A VAST CAVERN THAT LOOKED like something out of a nightmare. Candles flickered in nooks and crannies along the walls, casting dancing shadows across the ancient stone formations rising from the ground. In the center, an elaborate altar had been constructed from slabs, its surface covered in symbols that radiated evil. I swallowed heavily.

Virgil was bound to it with iron chains.

A tortured sound left Ellie at the sight.

"No," Gregory mumbled, his voice breaking.

The vampire had rocked to a stop a few feet ahead of us, shock rendering him immobile.

Virgil looked unconscious but alive, his chest rising and falling steadily. The iron chains looked cruel against the young vampire's pale skin, the dark stains on the stone beneath him telling their own grim story about what he'd suffered through since his abduction.

Beethoven's Ninth Symphony echoed through the cavern from speakers I couldn't see, the powerful music lending a macabre atmosphere to the horror in front of us.

"That sick bastard!" Ellie snarled, her eyes blazing red.

I followed her gaze, my heart thumping.

Ludvik stood with his back to us in the shadows at the far end of the cavern. He wore flowing dark robes and was completely absorbed in whatever he was reading from an ancient tome.

Samuel and I shifted, our wolves instantly recognizing the deadly threat he posed even though he seemed oblivious to our presence. The familiar heat of transformation flowed through me as I shook myself out, the change now as easy as breathing.

Gregory abandoned all pretense of stealth and charged across the cavern, his son's name a roar on his lips.

"*Virgil!*"

"No!" Barney barked, alarmed.

Ludvik spun around. His expression shifted from intense focus to mild annoyance.

"How tedious."

He moved faster than my eyes could track.

"Watch out!" Samuel shouted.

Gregory gasped when Ludvik appeared in front of him and backhanded him with enough force to send him flying into the cavern wall. Stone cracked from the impact.

Virgil blinked his eyes open on the altar. Confusion danced across his face as he tried to process what he was seeing. "Ellie, what are you doing here?!" His gaze found Gregory. Horror widened his eyes. *"Father!"* He struggled weakly against the chains binding him.

"He's coming!" Finnic warned.

Ludvik moved like fog, striking Samuel and Barney before either could react. My wolf grunted as a blow landed on my flank and sent me crashing into the dwarves.

Ellie's shriek of rage echoed through the cavern as she launched herself at Ludvik. The older vampire avoided her attack with inhuman grace and punched her in the face. Ellie staggered back a step, her head snapping sideways with a sickening sound.

She grabbed Ludvik's wrist and turned to face him.

"This stops now, you monster," she growled, her fangs gleaming in the gloom.

"Keep him pinned down!" Finnic shouted as he charged the vampire.

Ludvik wrenched himself free and was gone in the blink of an eye. The dwarf's axe skimmed the space where his neck would have been. Finnic cursed as the momentum spun him around.

My heart pounded as we regrouped in the middle of the cavern, our gazes frantically scanning the shadows. The air shifted to our left. Barney stumbled, fresh wounds appearing on his leg and arm where Ludvik had attacked him. A flicker of pain echoed across the mate bond and had my head snapping around. The sight of the claw marks on Samuel's shoulder made my wolf snarl with fury.

*I'm okay!* my alpha said, his fangs exposed and his hackles rising where he towered beside me.

"He's too fast!" Gregory's voice dissolved in a grunt of pain as he dropped to one knee, his hand rising to clamp the wound in his abdomen. The vampire's blood splattered thickly to the ground, the scent flooding my wolf's nostrils and causing Ellie to gnash her teeth.

Ludvik's next invisible attack sent Finnic flying into a cluster of candles, scattering wax and flame. The dwarf swore and shook his head dazedly as he climbed to his feet. Leoric, Belinda, and Wildred rushed over and took up defensive positions around him.

"The wraith's abilities!" Barney snapped. "He must be using them again!"

I looked around and spotted Bo, Didi, Gavin, and Mindy at the edge of the cavern. Just as we'd planned, they were searching the place for the wraith and the object Ludvik had used to bind her while we engaged the vampire, Melvina and Hilda assisting them.

"Mindy says she's struggling to sense her," Didi called out, magic crackling around her hands as she kept a lookout for Ludvik. "There's too much interference!"

Barney's eyes widened. "The music."

We met his stunned gaze.

"That's why he's using the music. To mask the wraith's presence!"

An unearthly wail erupted across the cavern, the sound coming from everywhere at once. Bo's ears flattened. Our breath began to mist as the temperature in the cavern plummeted.

"There!" Ellie pointed.

A pale figure had materialized near the altar,

translucent and with eyes full of pain and rage. My stomach lurched.

It was a little girl with a gaping hole in her chest where her heart should have been. She was hunched over and clawing at her head.

Fury burned through my veins.

Mindy flickered alarmingly, horror etched in every line of her face.

"A child," she mumbled. "He bound a *child*?!"

The wraith turned toward us, mouth opening in another bone-chilling scream that sent the dwarves stumbling backward. I glimpsed fangs and a glint of crimson in her eyes.

*She's a vampire,* Samuel growled.

Ludvik blurred into view beside the wraith. The little girl flinched.

My wolf stilled and blinked.

A thin red chain had just shimmered into view. It connected the wraith to Ludvik.

*Is that the binding?!*

Samuel shot a confused look at me. *What binding?*

"Can anyone else see that crimson line connecting that bastard to his ghost?!" Ellie asked in a low voice.

Barney and Gregory looked equally perplexed at her words.

"I can," Mindy ground out. The ghost was scowling.

My heart raced. Mindy, Ellie, and I were the only ones who could see the connection.

"We need to find the binding object." Frustration made Mindy's eyes glow. "It has to be here somewhere!"

She was right. It was the only way to slow Ludvik's insane speed so we could stop him. I lowered my head and curled my lips on a threatening growl as I approached the altar.

Ludvik sneered. "You can try all you want. You'll never find it." He cocked his head to the side, his expression mocking. "Now, how about I kill you all? Your bodies will make a nice offering for this ritual."

I braced as he vanished.

His attacks when they came were even faster than before.

My wolf detected the change in the air next to me a fraction of a second before he struck. I jumped, narrowly missing the claws aimed at my eye.

Power rolled off Ellie and Barney as they leapt, their faces dark with bloodlust. Ludvik grabbed them by the throat and hurled them across the cavern. They struck the wall hard and plummeted to the ground.

Samuel sprung, Gregory coordinating with him. Ludvik flickered out of view just as the wolf's fangs and the vampire's claws were about to carve his chest and back open. He reappeared beside them, took hold of their heads, and smashed their skulls together.

The sound made my wolf whimper.

Samuel and Gregory dropped to the floor with a groan. Blood streamed from a gash on my alpha's forehead as he struggled to rise, the sight making my stomach clench with dread. Gregory shook his head dazedly and tried to get back up, his temple bleeding where his skin has broken.

There was movement behind them.

Finnic dashed past with a throaty ululation. He leapt and managed to land a glancing blow on Ludvik's arm.

The vampire scowled at the sight of the thin line of blood blooming on his skin. He backhanded the dwarf violently across the face. Finnic went flying into Samuel and Gregory, taking them to the ground again.

The rest of the dwarves attacked, their battle cries rending the air.

Virgil's shout had my head snapping around.

"The base of that wall!" The vampire indicated the left side of the cavern with an urgent tilt of his head, the chains rattling around him. "He hid something there!"

I watched as Mindy, Bo, Didi, and Gavin headed swiftly to the location he'd indicated. Ludvik snarled and made to attack them.

I moved, my wolf letting loose a bloodcurdling sound.

Ellie got to Ludvik first, her figure moving so fast my pulse spiked.

"Oh no, you don't!" She grabbed him by the throat and lifted him off the ground before he could vanish.

I was beside her in an instant, my heart slamming against my ribs.

# CONSECRATED GROUND

"I CAN'T SEE ANYTHING!" DIDI'S HANDS MOVED frantically over bare stone as she and Gavin examined the cavern wall.

Bo whined with frustration and sniffed jerkily along the base of the wall. "There's definitely something here." He clawed at a thin crack.

Mindy dove headfirst into the wall.

Barney, Samuel, Gregory, and Finnic moved behind Ludvik and grabbed his arms, trapping him in place.

Ludvik's expression turned ugly. "You have no idea what you're doing!"

Mindy reappeared. "Found it!" She turned to Gavin, excitement lighting up her face. "Can you break the wall right here?!"

Gavin's tail popped out. The dragon newt twisted and smashed the wall with it. Stone crumbled. Something small and dark became visible in the candlelight.

Bo squeezed his muzzle into the gap and snatched it up in his jaws.

It was a doll. An old-fashioned one with a porcelain face, a faded dress, and a missing arm. The kind of toy that would have been precious to a little girl centuries ago.

My blood chilled as I recalled the strange message we'd found scrawled in the hidden room in the Chamber of Commerce subbasement. My head snapped to the wraith.

Tears streamed down the vampire child's face.

She had been trying to tell us how to free her all along.

Ludvik's composed mask finally cracked. *"No!"*

He broke free of Ellie and the others' holds, desperation giving his already inhuman speed a new edge.

My heart lurched. I leapt to stop him.

*Bo!*

The Husky flinched and looked at me, like he'd heard my wolf's shout. My fangs sank into Ludvik's shoulder with a vicious sound.

He shrugged himself free with a power that made my jaws ache.

Then the vampire was on Bo.

The Husky tried to dodge as Didi fired off magic and Gavin let loose a stream of fire to stop Ludvik.

The vampire evaded their attack.

His claws caught Bo across the side. The Husky yelped and went flying into the wall under the force of the strike, the doll still in his jaws.

There was a sharp crack. Bo dropped limply to the ground.

My pulse stuttered.

Mindy, Didi, and Gavin rushed to my dog's side. Bo stayed still for a moment before slowly struggling to his feet. A whine left him as he favored his left side. He was hurt but alive.

That small mercy was the only thing that kept me from losing myself completely to the rage engulfing me. I shifted back to human form and let the fury guide me, just like the time at the hospital. Heat unlike anything I'd ever felt before flooded my veins. My flesh shifted. I felt my face change and my hair lengthen.

When the transformation finished, I stood in my humanized wolf form—taller than my normal height, white hair cascading down my back, and the power flowing through every muscle so fierce my bones fairly vibrated with it.

The cavern, once so big, now felt small, like a space I could easily conquer in a few strides.

"What the—?!" Finnic mumbled. His axe struck the floor with a dull thud as his arm went limp at his side.

Gregory and Barney stared at me, wariness and shock warring in their crimson gazes. I felt Samuel's wonderment and admiration as he watched me where he still stood in his wolf form, his feelings sparking across the mate bond.

Something else sparked across my consciousness, startling me.

I looked at Ellie.

I could sense her power too, somehow. It was

different from Samuel's werewolf energy. Colder, sharper, but just as fierce. And for reasons I couldn't explain, her abilities appeared similar to mine.

"Is that you?" Ellie breathed, meeting my gaze.

I swallowed and nodded.

Determination tightened my best friend's face. "Let's finish this. Together."

We moved as one.

Ludvik snarled, his pupils flaring crimson.

I came at him from his left while Ellie struck from his right, our attacks perfectly synchronized, as if we'd fought together for years instead of minutes.

Ludvik tried to escape using his enhanced speed.

We were everywhere he wanted to be, boxing him in with movements that flowed like a deadly dance.

"Finnic!" Didi shouted. "Your axe!"

Finnic lobbed his weapon across the cavern.

Didi jumped and snatched it handle-first in midair.

Ludvik cursed and tried to bolt.

My claws raked his back while Ellie's fangs found his shoulder.

"Make sure you burn the doll!" I shouted at Didi. "It's the only way to fully break the hold he has on the wraith!"

Ludvik thrashed between me and Ellie, incoherent sounds of rage leaving him.

"Right, then." Didi narrowed her eyes and raised the axe. "One possessed toy, coming right up." She brought the weapon down on the doll.

The porcelain face shattered with a sound like

breaking glass, the pieces scattering across the cavern floor.

"Gavin!" the witch barked.

"On it!" Gavin inhaled and blew out a jet of white-hot flames that incinerated every last fragment of the cursed toy.

The effect was immediate and dramatic.

The crimson chain connecting Ludvik to the wraith child snapped like a severed rope.

The music stopped.

The little ghost girl blinked where she'd curled up on herself next to the altar, her eyes clearing of the pain and rage that had clouded them.

For a moment, she looked almost peaceful.

She slowly straightened and turned toward Ludvik, her expression shifting to something far more terrifying than mindless fury.

"You," she hissed in a voice like winter wind. "You hurt me. You made me hurt others!"

"No," Ludvik mumbled, his face went white.

I blinked as I felt the vampire's strength leaving him.

"I gave you power," Ludvik blubbered. "I gave you purpose—"

The wraith narrowed crimson eyes. "You gave me pain."

She moved faster than even Ludvik could, her ghostly form passing through Ellie and me to reach him. We gasped at the icy feeling.

The wraith's touch drained Ludvik of color. His eyes rolled back in his head and he screamed. Ellie and

I let go as he dropped to the ground and curled up on himself, his scream fading to incoherent blubbering.

The wraith studied him dispassionately for a long moment before looking around at all of us.

"Thank you." Her grateful gaze lingered on Mindy. "I can rest now."

My throat tightened as she faded away like morning mist.

The power that had kept me in my humanized wolf state retreated along with my rage. I shrank back down to my regular human form and slowly flexed my hand. Getting used to this new ability was not going to be easy.

A low groan distracted me.

Finnic had come over and kicked Ludvik.

Ellie and I stared.

The dwarf chieftain shrugged. "Just in case."

The other dwarves took this as a sign and came over to kick the vampire with undisguised enthusiasm.

"Should we stop them?" Ellie asked warily.

Her rage had started to subside and along with it her strange power.

She looked like my best friend again, albeit with fangs and red eyes.

I grimaced. "We might suffer collateral damage if we interfere."

Gregory and Barney headed to the altar to free Virgil. Ellie joined them while I went over to Bo.

Samuel shifted back to his human form and tagged along with me.

"How is he?" I asked Hilda anxiously.

"He's got a cracked rib," the dwarf announced where she was tending to the Husky. "He'll be fine with some rest."

Bo wagged his tail weakly. "I did good, right?"

Samuel smiled. "You did amazing, mutt."

I squatted and kissed my dog's head, my hands trembling with relief. "Next time, you're staying home."

"What and let you guys have all the fun?" Bo protested. He winced. "Ow."

A heavy scraping noise drew everyone's gaze.

Melvina appeared from the shadows beyond the altar. She was dragging something behind her.

"I found the coffin," the dwarf announced cheerfully. "It was in a chamber back there."

We all stared at the ornate coffin she was hauling.

Ludvik flinched where he was hugging the ground. He looked up jerkily.

"No," he wailed, his wild-eyed gaze locked on the wooden box. "Not the coffin!"

Barney's eyes gleamed with satisfaction. "Here will do, Melvina." He indicated the ground next to the altar.

Melvina beamed. "Right you are, Master."

"Please, Uncle Barnabas!" Ludvik pleaded, his voice quaking with terror. "I promise I'll disappear. You'll never see me again, I swear it!"

Barney watched his great-nephew coldly as he crossed the cavern. "That's what you told the vampire courts in Europe several hundred years ago. And yet, here we are."

Ludvik blubbered as Barney grabbed him by the collar and dragged him to the altar.

Melvina began removing stakes from her chain mail.

"Er, Barney," I said hesitantly. "Aren't you forgetting something?"

"Yeah," Didi muttered. "We ain't got no virgin blood."

Barney frowned. "What do you mean? We've got plenty." He indicated the blood stains next to the altar. "I could tell by the smell when he gave his blood to Ellie."

We stared. Our gazes rose as one to Virgil.

The vampire froze where he was sitting on the edge of the altar and rubbing the chain marks on his wrists.

"What?" he asked suspiciously.

"No way," Samuel muttered.

"You wouldn't think so, looking at that face, huh?" Finnic grunted.

"Seems you really can't judge a book by its cover," Didi said pensively.

Gavin's nostrils smoked. "He was a shy boy even at school."

Gregory patted his son's back, his expression a mix of parental love and manly sympathy. "My sweet child."

Ellie's eyes gleamed with an unhealthy light. "Boy, is he in for a wild ride," she said under her breath.

I grimaced at the thought of Virgil's cherry being popped by my best friend, AKA the new horny super-vampire in town. On the list of problems to have, it seemed pretty minor compared to the fate he'd almost suffered.

It took a moment for Barney to explain to Virgil

how one truly staked a vampire. Virgil flushed and covered his face in his hands.

"I can't believe this is happening," he mumbled.

Gregory hesitated. "Should we have that birds and bees conversation we never had when we get back home?"

"Father!" Virgil snapped.

"So all we need is a prayer, right?" I asked Barney while Finnic's warriors tied Ludvik up, gagged him, and dumped him inside his coffin.

"I may have muttered something along those lines when I thought we were all going to die earlier," Didi admitted.

We traded glances while Melvina administered a surreptitious kick to Ludvik.

"That works," Barney said with a shrug. "Who wants to do the honor?"

Ellie and I raised our hands.

Barney handed us some stakes while Leoric and Wildred manifested a pair of hammers from somewhere on their person.

Ludvik's eyes bulged with genuine fear as we grabbed the coffin lid and prepared to lower it.

"Wait," I said.

Ellie paused.

I put a hand out to Melvina. "I'd like a pair, please."

Melvina blinked. Her face brightened. She handed me a pair of googly eyes.

I stuck them to the inside of the lid, right where Ludvik would be staring for the rest of eternity.

Gregory sucked air between his teeth. "Oh, that's vicious."

"I like it," Finnic said smugly.

Samuel grinned. "Babe."

Bo sat down and wagged his tail. "Wait till I tell Fur Ball about this!"

"Any last words?" I asked Ludvik pleasantly as we prepared to close the coffin.

An inarticulate gurgle left Ludvik.

I raised an eyebrow. "Is that so? Well, Happy Eternity, asshole."

Ellie and I dropped the lid on Ludvik's choked scream and staked the coffin down.

# NEW ARRANGEMENTS

COMMITTEE ROOM A TURNED OUT TO BE NOTHING LIKE the formal conference room where we'd held our previous Alliance meetings. Instead of a polished table and rigid chairs, the space felt like a supernatural gentleman's club—leather armchairs, soft lighting, and a fully stocked bar that Finnic had already raided with the enthusiasm of a dwarf on a mission to get totally wasted.

"To victory!" the dwarf chieftain declared, raising his third tankard of the evening. "And to not dying horribly in a mine."

"To not dying horribly!" Melvina cheered, Hilda and the other three warriors joining in with raucous ululations that made the lights tremble and Daria wince.

Didi lifted her wine glass. "I'll drink to that."

Gavin nodded firmly as he sipped a margarita, Detective Johnson holding a beer beside him.

Most of the Alliance had gathered for what Daria

had diplomatically called a "post-crisis debrief," but which felt more like a celebration. Even Oscar had emerged from his usual shadowy corner and was nursing what looked suspiciously like a Cosmopolitan.

"So," Wendall said, addressing the room in general while pointedly not looking at me, "I suppose we should acknowledge that perhaps our initial skepticism was premature."

I raised an eyebrow. "Is that an apology?"

"It's an admission of tactical error," he replied stiffly.

I looked at Samuel, who shrugged.

"I'll take it," I said grudgingly.

Oscar cleared his throat from his zone of murkiness. "For the record, I also may have been hasty in my judgments."

"You tried to have her thrown out of her first Alliance meeting," Melody pointed out sharply.

Oscar avoided everyone's eyes and took a large gulp of his pink drink.

Finnic grinned smugly. "Some of us had the good sense to back the right horse from the beginning."

Titania narrowed her eyes. "You were drunk during her first Alliance meeting."

"He was drunk during *all* her meetings, including this one," Portia corrected.

"Are they always like this?" Detective Johnson hissed at Finnic.

The dwarf hiccuped and nodded.

Daria sighed and poured herself another vodka.

Pearl looked supremely satisfied with herself where

she lounged across the back of Victoria's chair. "The rest of you simply lack proper judgment." She swished her tail lazily. "I could tell how powerful Abby was when I first laid eyes on her."

Hugh, Ellie, and I exchanged a loaded look at this barefaced lie.

Even Victoria had the grace to look embarrassed.

"Says the cat who spent most of the battle sleeping on Victoria's lap," Barney murmured as he drank his Bloody Mary.

"I was recharging my batteries," Pearl said without missing a beat.

"For what?" Cornelius asked skeptically.

The cat blinked lazily. "To point out what you people did wrong."

"I didn't do anything wrong," Bo protested from the cushion at my feet. "I helped catch the bad guy!"

"So we heard," Daria said drily.

"Good doggie," Pearl added with the condescension of a queen.

Cornelius's mouth had flattened to a thin line.

Victoria sipped her whiskey with the expression of a woman determined to ignore her supernatural pet's diplomatic infractions.

Samuel took the chair next to mine, a martini in hand. He looked more relaxed than I'd seen him in weeks.

"So what's the official Alliance position on recent events?"

Daria consulted a tablet that contained proper notes rather than the ones with the doodles she let slip in official Alliance meeting minutes. "Ludvik Bludworth has been neutralized as a threat to Amberford's supernatural community. The ritual sites are in the process of being cleared and cleansed. The stolen materials have been recovered and are scheduled to be destroyed."

Detective Johnson nodded a confirmation at the latter statement.

Constantia's gaze flicked toward me and Ellie. "And the new developments?"

"Dear," Gregory protested weakly.

Virgil frowned at his mother.

I swallowed a sigh. Here it came.

"Ah, yes," Daria said awkwardly. "About that."

The room grew quieter, though Finnic continued humming what sounded like a drinking song under his breath. Detective Johnson fidgeted nervously in his chair.

"Your abilities," Portia told me and Ellie carefully. "They're rather…unprecedented."

"So I've been told," I replied.

Melody watched me closely. "The question is, what do they mean for the balance of power in Amberford?"

"Nothing," I said levelly. "I'm not interested in changing any balance of power. To be honest, I just want to go home and pretend the last week didn't happen."

Ellie spoke up from beside Virgil. "Same goes for me." She jutted out her chin. "I didn't ask to be turned into a vampire. Especially one with freaky powers."

"You have to understand that pretending none of it

ever happened isn't going to be possible," Daria said steadily. "What you and Abby demonstrated in that mine"—she glanced around the room—"well, it changes things."

"It might change people's expectations of us," I corrected with narrowed eyes. "It doesn't change who we are."

"No," Cornelius said, "but you have those powers nonetheless."

Finnic spoke up.

"The pair of them have proven remarkably effective at protecting this community," the dwarf grunted, raising his tankard.

The moment was ruined by his burp.

Though Samuel's face remained impassive, I could feel the tension humming through him across our bond.

"When push comes to shove, Amberford could use protectors like them." He looked at me and Ellie. "Not that I'm suggesting you sign up to the supernatural police force or anything." He grimaced at Detective Johnson. "No offense."

"None taken," the police officer muttered.

I studied the collection of faces watching me with varying degrees of hope, wariness, and calculation.

"If something threatens the people I care about, I'll deal with it," I said reluctantly.

"Fair enough," Daria said. "Miss Martin?"

"I'm still figuring out what being a vampire means," Ellie replied. "But Abby's right—if someone threatens my friends or family, they'll have problems."

"Speaking of family." Gregory brightened. "There's something Virgil wanted to announce."

Constantia gave her son an encouraging nod.

Virgil flushed slightly under everyone's gaze. "Ellie and I are moving in together."

Bo's head shot up.

My mouth went dry. "Moving in where?" I said numbly.

Ellie gave me a guilty look. "Well, we did talk about me moving into his place at first, but our apartment is bigger."

"Oh."

An awkward silence followed.

Victoria fixed me with a stare that spelled trouble. "Now's a good time to reconsider moving in with us."

Pearl swished her tail. "Victoria's right."

My palms grew clammy.

"She looks like she's gonna bolt," Detective Johnson told Didi and Gavin.

Samuel sighed at my hunted expression. He put his glass down and took my hands. "Moving in with me doesn't mean surrendering who you are, Abby. I think this will be good for us."

It was right up there at the top of the list of the scariest things I'd ever been asked to consider, but I decided not to tell him lest I hurt his feelings.

"I mean, I really don't see why you're making such a big fuss about this," Didi muttered. "It's gonna happen anyway, whether you like it or not. Such is the fate of mates."

"She's right," Barney said with a shrug.

I narrowed my eyes. "Fred has a betting pool going, doesn't he?"

The way Gavin flinched was all the answer I needed.

Oscar raised his Cosmopolitan before I could go super-werewolf on my coworkers. "To young love and questionable life choices."

"I'll drink to that too." Finnic clinked his tankard against Oscar's glass.

I pursed my lips, uncertain if I wanted my future happiness blessed by a demon and a drunk dwarf.

Samuel watched me with a hopeful expression.

"I won't say no to a trial period," I admitted reluctantly.

Bo perked up and wagged his tail enthusiastically. "Does that mean I get to be Fur Ball's roommate?"

Pearl squinted like she was suddenly having mixed feelings about this.

"Abby's a braver person than I am," Wendall muttered.

Samuel lowered his brows. "What's that supposed to mean?"

"She's moving in with your family," Wendall pointed out. "That includes Hugh."

"Fair point," Samuel admitted.

"I heard that," Hugh called out from where he was constructing some kind of layered drink at the bar. "I'll have you know I'm a delightful housemate."

"You set the kitchen on fire last month," Victoria said sharply.

"That was an accident," Hugh protested. "And it was a very small fire."

Victoria scowled. "The fire department disagreed."

My mouth pressed to a thin line.

I hadn't even moved in yet and I was already starting to regret my decision.

Samuel clocked my expression.

"No take backs," my alpha added hastily.

THE END

Abby and Bo's adventures continue in It's Raining Gargoyles. Coming soon!

Make sure to sign up to my store newsletter for special deals on my books and new release alerts. Or you can sign up to my author newsletter to get upcoming release notifications, sneak peeks, and giveaways.

# ACKNOWLEDGMENTS

To my friends and family. I couldn't do this without you.

To my readers. Thank you for reading How to Stake a Vampire. I hope Abby and Bo's second adventure didn't disappoint! If you enjoyed my book, please consider leaving a review on Goodreads or on the store where you purchased it. Reviews help readers like you find my books and I truly appreciate your honest opinions about my stories.

# BOOKS BY A.D. STARRLING

SEVENTEEN NOVELS

Hunted

Warrior

Empire

Legacy

Origins

Destiny

SEVENTEEN SHORT STORIES

First Death

Dancing Blades

The Meeting

The Warrior Monk

The Hunger

The Bank Job

LEGION

Blood and Bones

Fire and Earth

Awakening

Forsaken

Hallowed Ground

Heir

Legion

# ABOUT A.D. STARRLING

Visit Shop AD Starrling and buy all of AD's ebooks, paperbacks, hardbacks, audiobooks, and exclusive special edition print books direct.

Want to know about AD Starrling's upcoming releases? Sign up to her author newsletter for new release alerts, sneak peeks, giveaways, and more.

Follow AD Starrling on Amazon.

Join AD's reader group on Facebook
The Seventeen Club.

Check out this link to find out more about A.D. Starrling
Linktr.ee/AD_Starrling.

www.ingramcontent.com/pod-product-compliance
Lightning Source LLC
Chambersburg PA
CBHW062010190726
48283CB00002BA/634